LOCAL DALIT
CHRISTIAN HISTORY

ISPCK Contextual Theological Education Series-25

LOCAL DALIT CHRISTIAN HISTORY

Edited by

George Oommen
John C.B. Webster

ISPCK
2002

Local Dalit Christian History—Published by the Rev. Ashish Amos of the Indian Society for Promoting Christian Knowledge (ISPCK), Post Box 1585, Kashmere Gate, Delhi-110006 under the ISPCK Contextual Theological Education Series (CTE)-25.

First Published 2002

ISBN: 81-7214-702-3

Cover design: TONY SMITH

Laser typeset and cover design by **ISPCK,** Post Box 1585, 1654 Madarsa Road, Kashmere Gate, Delhi-110006, Tel: 3866323, Fax: 91-11-3865490. E-Mail–ispck@nde.vsnl.net.in, Publishing@ispck.org.in Internet-www.ispck.org.in

Contents

PREFACE

This book contains five essays which were originally written for a consultation on Local Dalit Christian History held at United Theological College in Bangalore late in January 1999. Since then they have undergone significant revision. In addition, we have added an introductory and a concluding essay which contain our reflections on some of the issues involved in writing local Dalit Christian history. These reflections are based on our research experience as well as on the discussions of the papers and proposals presented at the consultation.

One aim of the consultation and of this book has been to rectify what we consider to be a serious imbalance in the study of Dalit Christian history. Most of the studies available in book or article form have used the region as the basic unit of study. We thought that these needed to be supplemented with microstudies which used a single congregation, urban neighbourhood or village as the unity of study. We therefore invited friends from different parts of India who we knew to be interested in this subject to join the project. What emerged from the consultation are these five essays which use different approaches, treat different themes, and describe the changing experience of Dalit Christians in five different states of India. We commend these essays to our readers in the hope that they will not only enrich our understanding of both the Dalit and the Christian experience in India but also inspire others to write local Dalit Christian histories.

We wish to thank the South Asia Theological Research Institute (SATHRI) and its former director, Dr. K. C. Abraham, for providing the funding which made the original consultation possible; the Shiloh Baptist Church in New London, Connecticut, and its pastor, the Rev. Dr. Benjamin K. Watts, for John Webster's travel expenses for the consultation; the ISPCK for publishing this book; and Penny Webster for formatting the chapters for publication.

George Oommen
John C. B. Webster

SITES USED IN THE CASE STUDIES

CHAPTER 1

INTRODUCTION

George Oommen

This collection of articles on the localized experiences of Dalit Christians may be viewed within the larger framework of the recent historiography of Christianity in India. Many historians have made a conscious and systematic attempt to move away from mission-centred history towards a history of the Christian community itself. This was not a simple or easy shift from one to the other; instead it has been a complex process involving divergent approaches and even variations within those approaches. One such approach involved shifting from a mission-centred to a Church-centred history. Much of this proved to be institutional history, but it did include a search for the Indian character of a Church which has come into its own. This type of history was part of a post-colonial search by the Church in India to find its own personality. Two features of this historiography stand out. Firstly, the elite Christians who belonged predominantly to the high caste groups were placed on a pedestal. Their leadership, theological as well as ecclesiastical, was celebrated and glorified. This was not surprising; the history of the nation itself was being written from an elite perspective at that time and the writing of Christian history followed parallel lines. Secondly, the mass conversion of the Dalits and Tribals to Christianity was relegated to the margins of this history and historical writing on this subject did not move beyond the "mass movement" discourse commenced by the missionaries and perfected by Pickett in the 1930s. It was centred on the conversion of the Dalits and largely ignored their subsequent history, as can be seen in the standard textbooks of Indian Church history still in use.[1]

[1] C.B. Firth, *An Introduction to Indian Church History*, Mysore: Christian Literature Society, 1961, pp. 191-198; A. Meersman, "The

A related development was the departure from a purely nationalistic reading of Indian Christian history. This led, for the first time in the historiography of Christianity in India, to a shift of focus away from the Christian elite and dominant groups to the vast majority of Christian people who were involved in the historical formation of Christianity in India. Thus, Dalits who were the shapers of the mass conversion movements that played a major role in the Christian story, became the heroes of this kind of history, although they were not its exclusive focus.[2] The result was that Dalits found a significant voice within the mainstream historical discourse on Christianity in India in an unprecedented way. Issues related to caste categories and socio-religious factors, which provided the context of the Dalits' conversion to Christianity, were discussed extensively. The growth of the colonial economy, the Hindu renaissance, caste and Neo-Hindu movements were also perceived as significant formative factors. The removal of social disabilities and the humanizing effects Christianity had on these peoples were

Catholic Church in India since the mid-19th Century," and T. V. Philip, "Protestant Christianity in India since 1858," in H. C. Perumalil and E. R. Hambye, eds., *Christianity in India: A History in Ecumenical Perspective*, Alleppey, Prakasam Publications, 1972, pp. 253, 270-72; M. K. Kuriakose, *History of Christianity in India: Source Materials*, Madras: Christian Literature Society, 1982, pp. 229-230, 370-372.

[2] G. A. Oddie "Christian Conversions in the Telugu Country 1860-1900: A Case Study of One Protestant Indian Movement in the Godavery-Krishna Delta," *Indian Economic and Social History Review*, XII (January- March 1975), 61-79; John C. B. Webster, *The Christian Community and Change in Nineteenth Century North India*, Delhi: Macmillan, 1976; Duncan B. Forrester, *Caste and Christianity: Attitudes and Policies on Caste of Anglo-Saxon Protestant Missions in India*, London: Curzon Press, 1979; Sundararaj Manickam, *The Social Setting of Christian Conversion in South India*, Wiesbaden: Franz Steiner Verlag, 1979; J. W. Gladstone, *Protestant Christianity and People's Movement in Kerala: A Study of Christian Mass Movements in Relation to Neo-Hindu Socio-Religious Movements in Kerala, 1850-1936*, Trivandrum: Seminary Publications, 1984; G. A. Oddie, ed., *Religion in South Asia: Religious Conversion and Revival Movements in South Asia in Medieval and Modern Times*, New Delhi: Manohar, 1991.

elevated to the core of the historiographical discourse. Although complex social and historical processes were assessed, most of the studies finally viewed Dalit conversion movements as movements seeking self-dignity and saw processes of humanization in the Dalit conversion experience.

One of the interesting aspects of this historiographical approach was the reshaping of the way in which the European missionaries' role would be perceived. Instead of being obstacles to the proper Indianization of the Church, they were depicted as co-actors in the whole Dalit people's movement to Christianity. It is rather significant, as will be evident in the articles in this book, that in the chosen memories of present day Dalit Christians, missionaries are placed on a high pedestal as liberative agents. Although many historians have been highly critical of the missionary role in Christian expansion and in the colonial systems, the nostalgic memories the Dalit Christians hold about the missionaries, as against the present oppressive leaders and high castes within Christianity, is rather noteworthy.

Eventually Dalit Christian history emerged as a legitimate and autonomous branch of study in its own right, rather than as an auxiliary to the study of some other aspect of the history of Christianity in India.[3] The methodological rationale for this was simple. Dalits constitute the majority of Christians and their history needs to be understood for its own sake and for their sake. In this type of history the subjectivity of the Dalit Christian experience has been unravelled in an unprecedented manner and their past voices, so long silenced, have been recovered.[4] The first study of

---

[3] See John C. B. Webster's pioneering and most comprehensive study, *The Dalit Christians: A History*, New Delhi: ISPCK, 1992.

[4] See some of the recent attempts in this direction: Dick Kooiman, *Conversion and Social Equality in India: The London Missionary Society in South Travancore in the 19th Century*, Delhi: Manohar, 1994; George Oommen, "Dalit Conversion and Social Protest in Travancore 1854-1890" in *Bangalore Theological Forum*, Vol. XXVII, (September-December 1996), 69-84; George Oommen, "Strength of Tradition and Weakness of Communication—Central Kerala Dalit Conversion", in

this type used the region or denomination as the basic unit of study.[5] There then followed a history which was national in scope.[6] This collection of essays is the first to focus upon the history of a single village or congregation.

This autonomous reading of Dalit Christian history represents a clear departure from the previous perspectives of Indian Christian historiography. At the same time it needs to be developed in conjunction with a pluralistic reading of the history of the peoples in India, which includes Dalit Christians as constituting a substantial portion of the Christian community. This stands in marked contrast to the work of *Hindutva* ideologues like Arun Shourie who want to read (or reread, as they claim) the history of Christian missionary work and the various movements connected with it on the basis of a monolithic, resurgent understanding of the Indian nation and its culture. This rereading is the result of a fascist view of Indian religion and society with a bias towards *Hindutva Vada* and a demand that this be the only way to read the history of different movements in India. Everything outside of *Hindutva Vada* is anti-national, they hold. When writing history of Christian missions in India, Arun Shourie said, "I believe that the essence of the Indian people is their inner quest, and that this quest is and the means by which it is pursued are Hindu first and foremost." He then had this to say about Dalits and Northeast India with obvious reference to Christianity:

> ...a point that will become evident when we come to missionary
> work in areas like the North-East and among groups like "Dalits":
> I believe that the interests of India as a whole must take

Geoffrey A. Oddie, ed., *Religious Conversion Movements in South Asia: Continuities and Change, 1800-1900*, Richmond: Curzon Press, 1997, 79-95; Walter Fernandes, ed., *The Emerging Dalit Identity: The Reassertion of the Subalterns*, New Delhi: Indian Social Institute, 1996; John C.B. Webster, *Religion and Dalit Liberation: An Examination of Perspectives*, New Delhi: Manohar, 1999.

[5] Those by Oddie, Manickam, Webster and Gladstone cited in footnote 2.

[6] John C. B. Webster, *The Dalit Christians: A History*.

precedence—overriding precedence—over the supposed interests of any part or group, religious, linguistic or secular. I also believe that, given the fragile condition of the structure of governance at the moment, the movements which are currently afoot ostensibly to "liberate" and "empower" these groups may well break India, that they will eventually bring upon even those groups the consequences that Bhindranwale's terrorism—much lauded by the "Dalit" leadership, which in turn has been much lauded by the Church—brought upon the Sikhs.[7]

With these new approaches to the history of Christianity in India have come new methodologies designed to seek out answers to the new questions which those who use these new approaches are raising. As John Webster indicates in his concluding article, this goes beyond reading traditional mission sources as their missionary authors intended them to be read. It involves locating new sources, interrogating them in different ways, relating them to a variety of contexts, employing the techniques of oral history, and drawing upon such allied disciplines as anthropology and sociology in framing as well as in offering answers to one's leading research questions.

The following chapters cover approximately a century of change. The authors have sought to locate their small Dalit Christian communities within their respective socio-religious contexts, to discover not only what directions these communities have taken in steering themselves away from past degradations and deprivations but also how at the same time they have sought to sustain a sense of continuity in the midst of change. The most unique contribution of this volume, we hope, is that it draws its case studies from several distinct regions of India and weaves together a story about how Dalit Christians have been Christianized (interacted with Christian teachings and disciplines, belief systems and ecclesiastical structures), acquired a new identity, and at the same time dealt with the forces of modernity and the challenges of mobility.

---

[7] Arun Shourie, *Missionaries in India: Continuities, Changes, ʼnmas,* New Delhi: ASA Publications, 1994, 2 & 3.

By getting below the region as the basic unit of study in order to find out whether, how and why broader developments were being manifested at local levels, these authors have challenged some of the "conventional wisdom" about Dalit Christian history. For example, a common popular perception regarding Dalit Christians in India is that they have experienced more upward mobility than other Dalits because of the literacy, educational and welfare programmes of the Christian missionaries and churches. It has often been assumed that Dalit Christians actually seized those opportunities to great advantage and so have improved their material conditions. But has that, in fact, been true? Critically verifying some of these issues is central to understanding the present position or predicament of the Dalit Christian community who describe themselves as "twice" or "thrice alienated."[8] What makes up the continuing and yet changing experiences of a local Dalit Christian community which is, on the one hand, a participant in a larger social setup and, on the other hand, struggling to hold on to Christianization processes and the new sense of identity that has given to them, are some of the issues which this study concentrates upon. Four major themes seem to emerge out of the local experience of the Dalit Christians which deserve special attention in this introduction. These are memory, identity, mobility, and fragility.

MEMORY

In the reconstruction of the Dalit Christians' historical past, their own selective memory plays a vital role. To fully understand and recapture a Dalit Christian congregation's or community's life

---

[8] See K. Wilson, _The Twice-Alienated: Culture of Dalit Christians_, Hyderabad: Booklinks Corporation, 1982. Some of the following studies provide historical and sociological background: James Massey, _Dalits in India: Religion as a Source of Bondage or Liberation with Special Reference to Christians_, New Delhi: Manohar, 1995; James Massey, _Downtrodden: The Struggle of India's Dalits for Identity, Solidarity and Liberation_, Geneva, WCC Publications, 1997; Godwin Shiri, _The Plight of Dalit Christians—A South Indian Case Study_, Bangalore: Asian Trading Corporation, 1997.

experience, therefore, we must examine the "facts" in order to ascertain whether those facts are accurate or whether they are constructed as status enhancing myths. A grasp of these myths and chosen memories is essential to make sense of the nature and sequence of local Dalit Christian history. Both the actual and the illusory dimensions of these memories are integral parts of their subjectivity, whether present or past; part of their creative agency involves selecting and/or creating a usable historical past and we as historians must discover how they did this if we are to do justice to our reconstruction of their Dalit Christian past. For example, there are Dalit Christians who have chosen to remember and glorify the self-sacrificing and life-giving involvement of missionaries in their conversion and they weigh that against the continuing upper caste hegemony embedded in the Christian structures. In this process other important aspects of their past might be distorted or neglected. Nonetheless, this selectivity in memory continues to influence the communities' history and present identity. Both Christian and other Dalits have a rich history of remembering their past through orality and they continue to sustain and shape it through oral tradition. The histories in this book rely heavily upon information gathered from orally transmitted community and individual memories. Dr. Dayanandan's chapter devotes considerable space to examining the historical basis of one such memory, that concerning the attitudes and actions of the Scottish missionaries in the Madras area towards caste and untouchability.

IDENTITY

The identity of Dalit Christians, i.e., their social positioning as both they and others perceive it, is one of the pivotal issues in these chapters. Historically, the experience of Christianization led Dalit converts to break, in varying degrees, with their *jatis*. This break, especially during the first generation, could be traumatic. As Daniel demonstrates through the experience of the Turkman Gate Christian community of Delhi, bonds of social integration were severely weakened when some decided to join this new religion and accept its demands. But they took the plunge anyway.

The psychological effects of this initial rupture and the Christianization process itself created a distinction between Christian and other Dalits, even while they lived side by side or mingled in the same neighbourhood. In different regions Dalit Christians struggled in varied ways to distinguish themselves as belonging to a community distinct from their *jatis* through education, lifestyle changes, the acquisition of land, as well as imbibing Christian values and piety. Christianity, education, and mobility appear to have played a definitive role in the formation of this emerged identity. However, this has very clearly created another dilemma for them. Many Dalit Christians struggle to relate to their own community members who are not Christians, in some cases their own kith and kin, especially in the present context of growing Dalit unity and solidarity, which may be identified as a process of Dalitization[9] (a common consciousness emerging out of their past experiences of socio-religious marginalization and deprivation based on their "untouchable" status).[10]

Most Dalit Christians show tenacity and determination in holding on to their Christian identity, even when they realize that Scheduled Caste privileges are denied to them because they are Christians.[11] However, some, as Oommen, as well as Hans and

---

[9] See also A. M. Abraham Ayrookuzhiel, "The Ideological Nature of the Emerging Dalit Consciousness", in A. P. Nirmal, ed., *Towards a Common Dalit Ideology*, Madras: Gurukul Lutheran Theological College & Research Institute, n.d; Bhagawan Das and James Massey, eds., *Dalit Solidarity*, New Delhi: ISPCK, 1995.

[10] This is a pan-Indian phenomenon that started with the initiative of the Dalit Panthers of Maharashtra. Self-assertive and militant political action is integral to this movement. One major expression of their solidarity is Ambedkarism, an ideology based on the socio-political teachings of Dr. B. R. Ambedkar. See Gail Omvedt, *Dalits and the Democratic Revolution: Dr. Ambedkar and the Dalit Movement in Colonial India*, New Delhi: Sage Publications, 1994; Eleanor Zelliot, *From Untouchable to Dalit: Essays on the Ambedkar Movement*, New Delhi: Manohar, 1996.

[11] Brojendra Nath Banerjee, *Struggle for Justice to Dalit Christians*, New Delhi: New Age International, 1997. For an historical discussion

Macwan have pointed out, left Christianity or resorted to a dual religious identity in order to overcome this dilemma. In fact, the issue of identity becomes very complex among Dalit Christian communities depending on the regions they come from. In the Gujarat situation, urban Christians who are economically mobile refuse to be identified with the "outcaste" or "backward" label and resent being reminded of social roots they would like to forget. So, despite the strongly emerging Dalitization, or militant Dalit consciousness, among Dalit Christians this historic dilemma of Dalitization verses Christianization still persists. Shiri as well as Hans and Macwan identify these problems and Shiri observes that urban Christians in Karnataka are refusing to avail themselves of the "Other Backward Class" facilities provided by the state because they wish to hide their untouchable origins behind their Christian identity. Among both the Gujarati and the Kannadiga communities studied, there is an exclusivism developing among Dalit Christians, especially when questions of marriage and inter-dining are involved. In this context the observation of Hans and Macwan about the Gujarat situation is sociologically significant: "In the case of the city Christians religious identity takes precedence over the caste identity while in the villages the caste and the religious identity compete with one another." While competing identities cause a dilemma for Dalit Christians, particularly when they hide or reject their Dalit identity or when that is public knowledge, on the whole they are being increasingly but gradually accepted into the higher social status groups more readily than other Dalits in all the cases studied.

Almost all the case studies observe that the strong desire and the struggle to establish a "Christian" identity for Dalits still continues. Sometimes their identity is contested and at other times dual identity creates psychological tensions within and for the

of this issue, see John C. B. Webster, *The Dalit Christians: A History* (1992) 129-190., Jose Kananaikil, *Christians of Scheduled Caste Origin*, New Delhi: Indian Social Institute, 1983; Jose Kananaikil (ed.), *Scheduled Castes in Search of Justice. Part II: The Verdict of the Supreme Court*, New Delhi: Indian Social Institute, 1986.

community. While it appears that almost all the Dalit Christian communities we have studied have established their distinct identity as against other communities present around them, the stigma of untouchability has not completely disappeared. The community deals with this at times silently and other times assertively. For instance, Dalit Christians in Kerala assert their right to a dignified identity in the larger social setting by opposing preferential treatment of the Syrian Christians within the Church, while the Dalit Christians in Gujarat have accepted this situation of helplessness with a certain amount of resignation.

MOBILITY

As noted earlier, regional and national level studies of first generation Dalit converts have demonstrated that the dominant motivation which drew them to Christianity was their search for human dignity and self-esteem. Our study reveals that Dalit Christians have travelled a long, arduous and at the same time a meaningful journey towards firmly asserting their God-given sense of human dignity in the face of dehumanizing forces. Winds of change have obviously been moving in the society and in their own lives. Several of the resources that Christianity offered them seem to have provided an impetus for bringing out the best in them. Literacy and education were especially helpful to all Dalit Christians in gaining some mobility, but have not been a panacea. Their desire to make of themselves something more than what the surrounding society considered them capable of becoming has always been frustrating and usually incomplete. What they have actually achieved in terms of position in the local social milieu is quite complex.

While all Dalit Christians seem to have experienced some form of social and occupational mobility, urban Dalit Christians seem to enjoy a higher level of upward mobility and resultant acceptance from other higher social status groups, including upper caste Christians, than their rural counterparts. In Godwin Shiri's case study of the Dalit Christians of Mandya, a semi-urban and industrialized town, one can see that many moved to non-traditional industrial occupations within a short time. In Mandya after two decades of Christianization no Christian was found to be following their caste occupation of weaving. In fact, the most dramatic aspect of urban Dalit Christian upward mobility is their gradual but complete break from their traditional occupations. Shiri and Monodeep Daniel particularly emphasize this transition more than others. It is true that missionaries did acquire some agricultural land for Dalits here and there, as Hans and Macwan have shown, or they have subsequently acquired it on their own, but historically migration to the town or city has been the primary way in which rural Dalits have gained occupational mobility, whether they are educated or not. Moreover, the cases studied by Shiri, Oommen and Daniel all indicate that women as well as men have shared in this occupational mobility. The overarching picture that emerges from the case studies here is that of a general upward mobility among Dalit Christian communities in which literacy and schooling played the most decisive roles.

In this story of mobility another dimension comes across very clearly. While Christian Dalits had an advantage over other Dalits in the job market when the competitors were fewer in number and the Christian Dalits had a higher rate of literacy and better educational qualifications, the situation is now rapidly changing and the resulting picture needs to be redrawn completely. The exclusion of Christian Dalits from the government's reservation policy, which provides other Dalits with a definite percentage of job opportunities, has greatly disadvantaged them in the post-colonial history of India. Members of the Scheduled Castes can attain goals of mobility through these job reservations denied to Christian Dalits. The result has primarily been hardship, rejection and frustration. As Shiri says, there is stagnation and a high rate of unemployment among Dalit Christians as a result of this. Of course, it is a matter of concern that some Dalit Christians are refusing to claim to be "Scheduled Caste converts to Christianity" or "Other Backward Classes," as that would reinstate them into an untouchable identity. While this is understandable, it does add to the complexity of the issue because at present *Hindutva* forces are exploiting every opportunity to divide and rule the Dalit community in India by arresting the evolving Dalit consciousness and empowerment. The struggle all Dalits face between leaving and forgetting their untouchable past on the one hand, and developing a strong Dalit consciousness on the other, can be seen among Christian Dalits as well, since the 1970s and 1980s. In fact, this has been a pan-Indian tendency, although a subtle one. This issue has not come out clearly in our studies, but is implicit in several of them. The dilemma of the community which pulls them schizophrenically between Dalitization and Hinduization (a kind of co-option into Hinduism) needs further empirical study.

The gradual improvement in the inter-caste social acceptance and the consequent mutuality among the high caste and the Dalit Christians become apparent in the studies of Shiri, Oommen, Hans and Macwan. There is more inter-dining and movement between peoples within localities and particularly within the church circles. However, the last bastion to be conquered in this regard is inter-caste marriages between lower and upper status groups within Christianity. As elsewhere in society such transcendence of caste barriers is hard to come by. Nevertheless it should be noted that Shiri's study indicates an exceptional variation within the historical experience of Dalit Christians. Without much ado, many Mandya Christians are marrying Mangalore Christians who are generally perceived to be higher in social status than Dalit Christians. This relatively stable tie between two status groups in Karnataka could be explained by the income earning opportunities available to Mandya Christians.

Upward mobility is not just a result of access to resources made available by Christianity. Social movements and political action have also played a definite role. Though an important issue, these aspects have not been widely discussed in the articles in this book. Definitely literacy, education, the church building and the land, separately or in combination, have given Dalit Christians an impetus for pushing forward in life, not only leaving behind a past of degradation and deprivation but also sustaining a distinct identity of their own in a highly complex socio-cultural milieu. However, it should be noted, as Hans and Macwan observe in their study of

Gujarat as does Shiri in his study of Karnataka, that the domesticating power of Christianity on the lower strata of converts has, to a great extent, weakened their ability to take political action and resist human rights violations.

Notwithstanding the overall social improvement and economic mobility education has provided to Dalit Christians, few of them have been able to get higher level jobs. This has to be weighed against the greater success that upper caste elite Christians have made through Christian educational institutions in moving into the higher echelons of society and the high income generating occupations. The whole issue of education and upward mobility is viewed in a radically different way by Dayanandan after examining the experience of Dalit converts from Andreyapuram, located not far from perhaps the most prestigious Christian institution in South India, the Madras Christian College. His incisive analysis reveals in a powerful way how missionary educational policies were so discriminatory against Dalit Christians in denying them for over a century an educational opportunity through which they might move upward beyond a lower middle class or middle class level. While significant in terms of their Dalit backgrounds from which they had come, Dalit Christian mobility was very modest when compared to what upper caste Christians and Hindus were able to achieve through Madras Christian College. Whereas educated high caste Christians and other Hindus exploited Christian institutions to gain access to high income and status-earning occupations, Dalit Christians had to be content with jobs of lower status and income. According to Dayanandan, these highly educated elites, who include Christians of tremendous economic and social influence, have taken their anti-Dalit attitudes to further heights than the missionaries did.

In fact, Dayanandan's study shows another tragic side to the story of the Dalit Christians' upward mobility. Due to the ideological prejudice and policies of missionaries and the iron grip caste Christians continued to enjoy within the Church, Dalit Christians still remain behind other Christians. When it comes to the issue of overall upward mobility, they have had to be content with the broken bread pieces that fell down from the table. The continued denial of Scheduled Caste status to Dalit Christians, which is a clear discrimination on the basis of religion, has only added to this frustrating picture of their upward mobility. Important changes may occur in the overall life of a Dalit Christian community of a locality—type of residence, job, income, lifestyle—but these represent only modest advancement within the existing framework rather than a fundamental change in the basic social fabric. While emphasizing the brighter side of this comparative mobility of Dalit Christians, which did constitute a radical shift from their pre-existing occupational situations, we should neither forget nor play down the constraints to further mobility with which they have had to contend. Missionaries, as Dayanandan presents them, were both helpers (by sponsoring literacy and education) and hindrances (by putting a low ceiling on their rise) to Dalit Christian mobility. Whether this was as true of all missionary societies as it was of the Church of Scotland Mission in Madras bears further study. In any case, these findings give pause to those who assume that Dalit Christians were given "every advantage" by the missionaries and therefore do not need or deserve Scheduled Caste benefits. They also suggest that the theological and ideological fabric on which the missionary policies were framed were, at least at times, fraught with prejudices detrimental to the life experience of Dalit Christians. The exploitative and discriminatory type of casteist divide that is so apparent within Christianity in recent years is a historical consequence of missionary and upper caste Indian Christian prejudices.

FRAGILITY

All the studies in this book point to the fragile nature of Dalit congregations. The processes of disintegration, declining numbers, lack of emotional and substantive attachment to the congregations are manifestations of this fragility. This serious impasse in the historical experience of Dalit Christians has mostly been due to the Church's traditional neglect of the pastoral, ministerial, ritual and emotional needs of the people in these congregations. We may note that this has happened in spite of considerable social mobility among the people. The upward mobility of some Dalit Christians has disrupted the solidarity of local Dalit communities. When some leave the local community and move on to greener pastures elsewhere, thus reducing the traditional core group in size and strength, the local congregations or communities become more vulnerable and may even disintegrate due to a loss of their best potential leadership. While Christianization has given Dalit congregations a sense of identity, deprivation of systematic pastoral care has placed the congregations in a state of stagnation. Shiri observes that rural Dalit Christian communities receive less pastoral attention than do urban congregations. Dalit Christian families or groups become disaffected or join other sectarian Christian groups when adequate pastoral care is lacking. Some even seek active reconversion to Hinduism, but for the substantial majority this has not been an acceptable option. There is a sense of solidarity against all odds in the remaining community when the mobile leave. The tenacity with which Dalit Christians hold on to Christianity despite lack of pastoral care and sense of frustration in the hope for mobility is profound.

Whatever the duration of the Christianization process, rural Dalit Christians have moved between their pre-Christian belief systems and the Christian systems with an element of ambivalence. This is another manifestation of fragility. The search for the primordial experience of their ancestors has erupted in gross conflict with the existing Christian discipline of a congregation. As Oommen demonstrates in his study, such conflict leads to disruption and disintegration in the local Dalit Christian community. These and other forms of movement across religio-cultural boundaries are only part of a long-standing Dalit attempt to come to terms with the processes of Christianization that demand total loyalty to its beliefs, practices and discipline.[12]

---

[12] See for an analysis of similar phenomenon in an urban setting, Lionel Caplan, *Class and Culture in Urban India: Fundamentalism in a Christian Community*, Oxford: Oxford University Press, 1987.

The features of the rich social and religio-cultural experience of Dalit Christians include continuities and transformations, strengths and fragility. We hope that this book will be seen as an initiation into the study of local Dalit Christian communities and congregations, and that the complexities and variations found in these studies will stimulate further research. More studies of local Dalit Christian congregations and communities will definitely help to provide a clearer overall picture than we have at present. With this end in view, a methodological article by John Webster had been included in this collection. This seeks to bring together in a useable form some of what this group of authors have learned and shared with one another about the process of researching and writing local Dalit Christian history.

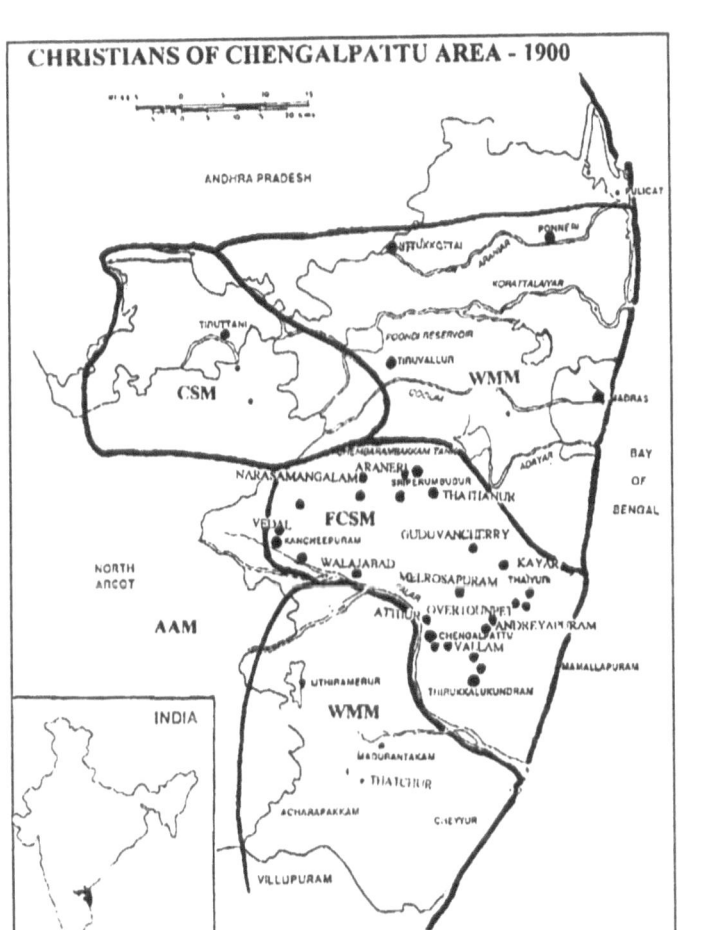

CHRISTIANS OF CHENGALPATTU AREA - 1900

CHAPTER 2

DALIT CHRISTIANS
OF CHENGALPATTU AREA
AND THE CHURCH OF SCOTLAND

P. Dayanandan

Andreyapuram is a sleepy little hamlet east of Chengalpattu. In 1892 several families of Dalit converts of the Free Church of Scotland decided to make this a place of hope and a new beginning. Although such exclusive Christian settlements are rare, the community here today is typical of numerous small Protestant congregations in Dalit sections of villages in northern Tamil Nadu. These Christians are the descendants of small groups of brave men and women who embraced Christianity in the erstwhile Chengalpattu, North Arcot and South Arcot districts. About one hundred years ago many Paraiyar leaders responded to the intense evangelistic work organized by the missionaries of the Free Church of Scotland Mission (FCS), the Established Church of Scotland Mission (CS), the Wesleyan Methodist Missionary Society (MMS) and the American Arcot Mission Society (AAM). Soon numerous small group movements to Christianity added to the religious diversity of this ancient countryside. The rural Protestant church is entirely Dalit in composition. Most of the descendants of the Dalit converts of the American Arcot Mission are now in the Vellore Diocese of the Church of South India (CSI). The regions evangelized by the other missions are now part of the Madras Diocese of the CSI. There are more than 600 congregations, 25,500 families and 84,000 Christians in the rural areas of the Madras Diocese, i.e. all villages and a few towns outside the city of Chennai.[1] Most

---

[1] The Madras Diocese now includes parts of Nellore and Chittoor districts of Andhra Pradesh in the north and extends south into

of these Dalit congregations have been in existence for 50-100 years.

One hundred years is a sufficiently long and opportune time to assess the life and progress of Dalit communities who converted to Christianity. This paper examines the early events of conversion in villages around Chengalpattu, and the subsequent crucial role of the Free Church of Scotland Mission in both opening up and denying opportunities and avenues of progress for the converts. Surprisingly, any other rural Dalit Christian community in northern Tamil Nadu region would tell a similar story: of village leaders helping to liberate their people from oppression; of the converts' remarkable appreciation for the spiritual and emancipating power of their new-found faith; of a few extraordinarily sensitive missionaries who identified themselves with the Paraiyar; of the slow progress of this community; and of the ever-present suppressive power of caste in their lives. This history of local Dalit Christians is inspired by and adds to John Webster's pioneering account of Dalits in India who found in Christianity a new faith, freedom, self-respect, dignity and hope of a better future.[2]

The setting seemed perfect for a true emancipation of the Dalit Christians of north Tamil Nadu. The city of Madras (now Chennai) was very close, with all that it could promise and offer —access to influential people, jobs, trade, transport, government, and courts. All major missionary societies had their leaders and representatives in the city of Chennai. By 1900 they had at their disposal a century

Pondicherry. The Diocesan Statistical Review of 2001 reported that in 2000 there were 189,918 Christians, 60,571 families, 832 congregations and 140 pastorates in the Diocese. Of these 84,061 Christians of 25,579 families, 638 congregations and 52 pastorates were in villages and a few small towns. 45% of the Christians lived in these rural areas. The remaining congregations and pastorates were in the city of Chennai and its immediate neighbourhood and they included local residents, Dalit Christians from the surrounding villages and others who have migrated from the southern parts of the State and Kerala.

[2] John C. B. Webster, *The Dalit Christians: A History*, second edition; Delhi: ISPCK, 1994.

of practical experience with and accumulated knowledge of the proven methods of conversion and nurturing the progress of converted Christian communities. Perhaps the most potent of all liberating forces for the new converts, namely a sound English education, was at their doorstep. The Madras Christian College (MCC), founded by the Church of Scotland, and at that time managed by colleagues of missionaries working among rural Dalits, had already established itself as the premier educational institution of South India, and a route to highly paid and influential positions.

APPROACH AND SOURCES OF INFORMATION

This study is born out of a desire of a descendant[3] of Dalit converts of the Free Church to make sense of one's own history. A drama of great significance unfolds to any descendant who cares to look back at the conversion of their ancestors, three to four generations ago. For hundreds of people in the district, conversion to Christianity was the beginning of a new history. The present account is partly personal, from the vantage point of origins in the Chengalpattu area, association with the FCS, and education at MCC; hence the choice and focus on places mentioned in this narrative. I grew up and had my early education in three villages associated with the FCS where my father was a teacher-catechist. Thus, parents, uncles, aunts, and friends who lived or served as teachers and catechists in several Christian villages, and the villagers themselves constitute the primary source of information for this account. The Sunday services, Wednesday family prayers, singing to the accompaniment of cymbals and *mirudhangam*, harvest festivals, Christmas celebrations, baptisms, marriages and deaths in the Dalit Christian villages are an intimate part of one's history and provide both insight and appreciation of the life of Dalit

---

[3] My mother's grandparents with their four children were converted and baptized by Rev. Adam Andrew on 25 March 1898 at Kayar. My father's grandparents were baptized on 7 December 1902 by Rev. J. H. Maclean near Sriperumbudur.

Christians of this region. During the past few years many retired teachers, pastors, family members (especially my mother), and elderly villagers have shared with me their memories of descendants of the early converts and the missionaries who converted them, of village life, and of the many interconnections that existed between people of all Dalit Christian villages. The present narration draws heavily on these unwritten oral traditions and personal knowledge. Written sources of information such as books and various contemporary mission records are cited in the footnotes.

A valuable document, the baptismal and burial register maintained by the Rev. Adam Andrew, surfaced in 1993 while I was preparing for the centenary celebrations of the St. Andrew's Church, Chengalpattu. It contains information about the date, name, age, caste and place of converts as well as the names of the people who baptized the converts between 1880 and 1898. This register covers a crucial period in the history of the FCS when Andrew witnessed group movements of Paraiyar in the Chengalpattu district. The contents of the register can be grouped under the following categories: (a) 1880 – 1890 Baptism of children of early Christians and caste Hindus (b) 1891 – 1898 Baptism of Paraiyar group movement converts, and (c) 1882 – 1896 Burial record of Christians.[4] The names and dates of Andrew's register take us back to the world of a people breaking the chains of more than a thousand years of oppression and seeking dignity and respect for themselves and their descendants.

The conversion of rural Dalits by Andrew was preceded by the establishment of a native church by Rev. John Anderson who

---

[4] The first entry of baptism was made on 26 May 1880, and the last on 18 December 1898. More than 790 baptisms are entered ranging over a period of 18 years and 7 months. About 60 burials are entered between 1882 and 1896. The Chengalpattu pastorate then included a large mission area of many villages in and around Chengalpattu, Walajabad, Kanchipuram and Sriperumbudur. The register records baptisms held at 31 villages, including Andreyapuram. This register will be reprinted shortly.

founded the Madras Mission in 1837.[5] About forty years before Andrew made his first entry in the baptismal register, Anderson had already baptized his first convert, P. Rajahgopaul on 20 June 1841. The register of the Madras Mission of the General Assembly of the Free Church of Scotland (1841-1863) is now in the archives of the United Theological College, Bangalore.[6] The 209 baptisms tell a story not of Dalits but of the conversion of the upper caste young men and women at the General Assembly's school founded by Anderson, and this source of information is of interest for our discussion on the role of caste in the life of the Dalit Christians of the Chengalpattu area.

In this study an attempt is made to understand the conversion of Dalits in the Chengalpattu area by examining the situation of the Dalits and the approach of the missionaries. What was the condition of the Dalits and why did they convert to Christianity?[7] What was the pattern of conversion? Who took the initiative in each village to convince their relatives and friends to convert? What was so compelling in the Christian message they were hearing for the first time that they could resolve to remove themselves so completely from their gods, myths, festivals and culture? What resources for progress were available to the converts? Were the events in and around Chengalpattu area representative of contemporary happenings in the adjoining fields of other missions? What was the ideological approach of the Scottish missionaries to the conversion of Indians in general and Dalits in particular?

The ministry of the FCS cannot be understood without an account of the role of Madras Christian College. The college work

---

[5] J. Braidwood, *True Yoke-Fellows in the Mission Field: The Life and the Labours of the Rev. John Anderson and the Rev. Robert Johnston*, London: James Nisbet, 1862.

[6] Anderson's register has 156 entries. This register seems to be incomplete; an additional 43 baptisms of this period, not found in this register, were described by a fellow missionary, Rev. John Braidwood in his book, *True Yoke-Fellows*.

[7] For a general survey on mass movements see J. Waskom Pickett, *Christian Mass Movements in India*, New York: Abingdon Press, 1933.

was seen as one of the major fields of the Free Church in Madras.[8] The college work is of particular interest in local Dalit Christian history because of the internal contradictions and disproportionate resource allocation within the Free Church missionary endeavour to the education of the upper caste youth on the one hand, and evangelism of the rural Dalits on the other. For these reasons the contributions of John Anderson, William Miller and Adam Andrew are discussed in some detail. The people, their conditions and events of the Chengalpattu area cannot be easily circumscribed and we must therefore touch upon, however briefly, some of the other regions such as Thiruvallur and Arakkonam, and the other missions that worked there.

PROTESTANT CHRISTIANS OF CHENGALPATTU AREA

The city of Chennai (Madras) was a major centre for about ten different Protestant missionary bodies.[9] In 1726, Benjamin Schultze founded the Madras Mission of the Society for the Propagation of Christian Knowledge. More missionary bodies entered and rapidly expanded their activities after 1813 when policy changes in the East India Company charter opened up British dominion for European missionaries.[10] The London Missionary Society, the Church Missionary Society and the Wesleyan Methodist Missionary Society organized small congregations in the city, with converts chiefly from the lower castes, and established many schools for boys and girls. The missionaries did reach out to the villages but with no significant results. As early as 1820 C. T. E. Rhenius of

---

[8] G. Pittendrigh and W. Meston, *Missions of the United Free Church of Scotland: Story of our Madras Mission*, Edinburgh: United Free Church, 1907.

[9] M.A. Sherring, *The History of Protestant Missions in India: From their Commencement in 1706 to 1871*, London: Trubner and Co., 1875. G. Houghton, *The Impoverishment of Dependency: The History of the Protestant Church in Madras 1870-1920*, Madras: Christian Literature Society, 1983, 1-7.

[10] *Ibid.*

the CMS and his successors established outstations in Pulicat, Chengalpattu and Kanchipuram.[11] These outstations were later abandoned when Rhenius moved to Thirunelveli where he achieved remarkable success among the Nadars. By 1860 there were probably no more than 3,500 Christians in the city of Chennai and a few or no Christians in the rural areas beyond Chennai. The native Christians in the city and Chengalpattu district increased to 5,085 in 1871 and to 6,874 by 1881.[12] Even at this stage there were only about 200 rural native Christians of all missions in the Chengalpattu district. By 1871 there were 112 Christian educational institutions with 8,252 pupils mostly in the city of Chennai. For reasons difficult to understand the rural people were not responding to evangelization up to this period.

The Dalit Christians of north Tamil Nadu owe their origins primarily to the evangelistic, educational and medical ministry of three major missionary bodies in the rural areas of this region (see map, p.16).[13] The Free Church of Scotland Mission was active in and around Chengalpattu, Sriperumbudur, Walajabad and Kanchipuram, while the MMS was engaged in regions around Thiruvallur, Poovirundhavalli and Madhuranthakam. Adam Andrew and William Goudie were the two most prominent missionaries associated with these two missions and places. A third locality, Arakkonam, Sholinghur and adjoining regions in the North Arcot district, west of Thiruvallur, was also associated with the Church of Scotland (CS).[14] This happened because of a split, known

[11] M. A. Sherring, *op. cit.*, 379.

[12] *Ibid.*, 400-401.

[13] Most of the adjoining South and North Arcot districts was the mission field of the American Arcot Mission of the Dutch Reformed Church of America. The Christians of this area, now in the Vellore Diocese too, are Paraiyar converts of similar social and economic background as the Christians of the Chengalpattu district. The Leipzig Evangelical Lutheran Mission established in 1848 converted a small number of Dalits in the Chengalpattu district. The Lutheran Christians did not join the Church of South India.

[14] This is, therefore, a source of confusion today to many Christians who are not aware of the history of the split and reunion of that Church.

as The Disruption within the Church of Scotland.[15] Before the Disruption, Rev. John Anderson had founded the Church of Scotland Mission in Chennai in 1837. When the Disruption occurred in Scotland Anderson and his fellow missionaries, Rev. Robert Johnston and Rev. John Braidwood, opted to join the Free Church of Scotland. The Established Church of Scotland had no mission presence until 1845 when three new missionaries arrived, Rev. James Grant, Rev. James Oglivie, and a teacher, Mr. James Sheriff. Those who followed them, particularly Rev. Henry Rice and Rev. Alexander Silver, made significant contributions in and around Arakkonam, Sholinghur, Nageri, Thiruthani and Vellore. For 84 years since 1845 the two missions worked side by side until, in 1929, the "breach was healed" in Scotland, and the United Free Church of Scotland (which came into existence in 1900 by the merger of the Free Church with the Presbyterian Church) and the Established Church were reunited into one Church of Scotland.[16]

CASTE, CONVERSION AND THE FREE CHURCH OF SCOTLAND

The story of the Dalit Christians of the Free Church must begin with the arrival of Adam Andrew and his wife in 1879, and the beginning of group conversions in 1891. The church was getting

This confusion is understandable since the Christians of the Chengalpattu, Kanchipuram and Arakkonam areas are now strongly interconnected by a common social heritage, marriage relationships, liturgy, employment, and involvement in the institutional and religious life of the Diocese of Madras of the Church of South India.

[15] A dispute over the relationship between the Church and the State in 1843 resulted in about one-third of the members and ministers separating from the parent Established Church and constituting the Free Church of Scotland.

[16] The Sholinghur area under the established Church of Scotland was transferred to the Australian Presbyterian Mission in 1912. The American Arcot Mission and the MMS also handed over some of their villages to the Australian Presbyterian Mission, and all these are also now part of the C. S. I. See B. Walpole, *Venture of Faith,* Madras: CLS, 1993, 143.

firmly rooted in the rural areas around Chengalpattu, Kanchipuram, Sriperumbudur and Walajabad. This was a Dalit church. Strangely, this was happening in spite of the wishes and strategies of the two most prominent persons connected with the FCS, its founder Rev. John Anderson and its famous Principal of Madras Christian College, William Miller, both of whom were appealing exclusively to youth from the upper castes in an urban educational setting. Indeed, caste and Christianity have an awkward association in the history of the Church of Scotland in South India and this should be explained before returning to Adam Andrew and the Dalit Christians.

Immediately after arriving in Chennai in 1837, John Anderson took charge of a school started by two Scottish chaplains. He moved the school from Egmore to the Black Town area, which had a larger population of caste Hindus, and commenced classes on 3rd April 1837 with 59 Hindu boys. Thirty years after Anderson, under the leadership of Rev. William Miller, the school began college classes, and in 1877 became the Madras Christian College.[17] Anderson's first grand aim was "conversion to God of the souls of his pupils."[18] He hoped for a college or a Normal Seminary where through English education a native agency of teachers, preachers and missionaries would be trained to "convey to their benighted countrymen the benefit of sound education, and the blessings of the gospel of Christ."[19]

Anderson was a prodigious worker. Just two years after the opening of the central institution in Chennai Anderson was opening branch schools in the city and distant places. A branch school was established in Kanchipuram on the 29th May 1839, and another one at Nellore in August 1840. The same year Anderson accepted

[17] For the history of Madras Christian College, see J. Braidwood, *op. cit.*; William Miller, "Historical Sketch," M.C.C. Calendar, 1899; W. Miller, *The Madras Christian College: A Short Account of its History and Influence*, Edinburgh: Macniven & Wallace, 1905.

[18] J. Braidwood, *op. cit.*, 62.

[19] *Ibid.*, 60-63.

an invitation from Judge Moorehead to take over a school he had started at Chengalpattu. It was to this school in Chengalpattu that Adam Andrew would come forty years later, and transform the life of many Paraiyar in the district. Another school was opened at Thiruvallur in 1857. The Thiruvallur branch school was later handed over to the Wesleyan Methodist Missionary Society in 1891. The Kanchipuram, Chengalpattu and Thiruvallur schools have been functioning uninterruptedly as the Anderson, St. Columba's and Goudie schools, and are now part of the Diocese of Madras of the C. S. I.

John Anderson's institution was immensely popular from the very beginning. All his students were from the upper castes and he deliberately did not seek out students from non-caste communities such as the Paraiyar. What good can come out of the lowly and the despised? The testing time arrived soon. In October 1838, just about a year and six months after the school was opened, three respectably dressed boys with usual "idolatrous marks of caste" on their foreheads were admitted to the school. After six days the other students discovered that they were Paraiyar, and with feelings of "aversion and detestation" demanded their expulsion from the school. Anderson stood firm on the principle of equality that he believed in. Although 100 of the 277 boys left the school, Anderson refused to expel the Paraiyar boys. Slowly the students started coming back. This often-quoted incident[20] is said to have influenced all Christian schools in Chennai to adhere to a policy of extending educational privileges to students of every community including the Paraiyar and other outcastes. It certainly revealed that as an individual, Anderson had high principles. However, this was of limited or no value to Dalits since no real efforts were taken to enrol outcaste students in schools offering English education.

This incident appears to be nothing more than a minor distraction from Anderson's goal of reaching the upper caste students. Johnston wrote in 1838, "Several Europeans had asked education for the sons of their Pariah servants. This was declined,

---

[20] J. Braidwood, *op. cit.*, 74, 77, 81.

not on the ground that they were Pariahs, but because the admission of a Pariah, however great an act of heroic charity it might appear, would disperse his caste pupils, and frustrate his great aim – the Christianizing of the untouched mass of the caste-bound population."[21] Five years later Anderson himself, while writing to the Ladies' Society in Scotland about the education of "pure Native females" had this to say:

> Pariah girls may be obtained in any numbers...Some of these girls have proved useful as ayahs;..."Well", the ladies may say, "are their souls not also precious—as those that have caste? Undoubtedly they are. But the problem to be solved is, How to reach the caste girls as effectively as the boys—a problem as yet undiscovered. If any Pariah girl, or any Christian girl, of the class above referred to, were educated, it would still remain unsolved. A wall of brass rises up between such and the caste girls not to be scaled or passed in the present state of the country.[22]

It is unfortunate that we have no information on the three Paraiyar boys. Who were they? Who were their parents? What motivated them to seek English education braving the consequences of their daring entry? And what became of them after they finished schooling? We also have no record of other Paraiyar students entering the school in later years. Perhaps the three young men were insatiably curious and had an irresistible desire to learn. Perhaps they sneaked in so they could go out with education that gave them self-respect and liberated them from the shackles of their oppressed status. The Scottish missionaries were well aware why the upper caste Hindu youth were flocking to their institutions where the Scriptures and Christian principles were taught daily. The students knew that English education "would soon become the main avenue to social distinction, to wealth, and power."[23]

[21] *Ibid.*, 75.

[22] *Ibid.*, 225.

[23] W. Miller, *Scottish Missions in India: Two Lectures*, Edinburgh, 1868, 22.

JOHN ANDERSON AND HIS CONVERTS

The conversions that Anderson had hoped for happened in 1841. Poovirundhavalli Rajahgopaul of the Mudhaliar caste and A. Venkataramiah, a Brahmin student, were baptized on 20th June. Both were 18 years old. The school went through a major upheaval, as happened again and again whenever a caste Hindu or Muslim student was baptized. Anderson, his fellow missionaries Johnston and Braidwood, and later the ordained converts, Rajahgopaul and Venkataramiah, together baptized 209 persons between 1841-1863. A total of 40 male and 68 female youth, some really children, were baptized during this period (Table 1). Except for 1843, 1852, 1856 and 1857 conversions were reported for every year, the minimum being 1 and the maximum 21 in 1854.

Table 1

CONVERTS BAPTIZED AT THE FREE CHURCH OF
SCOTLAND, MADRAS (1841-1863)

Total Number of Converts Baptized (Male & Female)	**108**
Number of Female Converts Baptized	40
Number of Male Converts Baptized	68
Children of Converts Baptized	81
Children of European Parents Baptized	20
Total Number of Baptisms	209

The converts came from several upper castes, as Anderson desired. They included Brahmins, Mudhaliars, Naidus, Chettys, and a few others such as a Nair or a Menon. Five of the converts were Muslims. Only one of the 108 converts appears to have been an outcaste. Quite a few were frequently backsliding; Anderson's house was full of drama and excitement at every conversion and apostasy.[24] Anderson and his fellow missionaries were strongly opposed to caste in the church[25] and laid great emphasis on the breaking of the caste on conversion. Their converts agreed that

[24] J. Braidwood, *op. cit.*
[25] *Ibid.*, 293-294.

caste was synonymous with Hinduism and idolatry and that their
break with caste was "final and irreversible."[26] On conversion the
sacred thread was removed, and *kudumi*, the tuft of hair, was cut
off. The ultimate symbol of breaking away from caste was the
converts sitting and eating at the same table with the missionaries.
Caste really was of no great consequence at this early stage in the
development of the native church. Indeed, it was one big family
with brotherly affection and sisterly love among the wives of the
converts.[27] Although the records are rather silent about it,
Rajahgopaul, Venkataramiah and Ethirajuloo probably married
Dalit Christian girls from other institutions[28] since the first
conversion of caste Hindu girls, five of them between ages 11 and
12 occurred only in 1847 after the three were married. Yet, there
was a glaring internal contradiction in Anderson's approach to the
downward spread of Christianity from the upper castes to the rest
of the Hindus. If the converts became casteless, how would anybody
recognize their origins? The converts thought of caste as a barrier
to the propagation of the Gospel and that any who retained caste
destroyed his own credibility, dishonoured Christianity and its
precepts, and confirmed the heathens in their idolatries.[29] Obviously
such converts themselves would never boast of their upper caste
origins while preaching the Gospel. One wonders if the missionaries
solved this problem subtly and cleverly by retaining the original
names of their converts. The male Hindu converts retained their
abjectly Hindu names, most of them associated with Hindu gods
(e.g., Venkataramiah, Ramanoojam, Govindarajooloo,
Parthasarady), and Muslim converts kept their Muslim names (e.g.,
Abdul Ali and Zynool Abideen.) Interestingly, except for a few, all
the female converts were baptized with Biblical or European names.

[26] D. B. Forrester, *Caste and Christianity: Attitudes and Policies on
Caste of Anglo-Saxon Protestant Missions in India*, London: Curzon
Press, 1979, 125-127.

[27] J. Braidwood, *op. cit.*, 318.

[28] For a general discussion on marriage among converts, see L. Caplan,
Religion and Power: Essays on the Christian Community in Madras,
Madras: Christian Literature Society, 1989, 124-126.

[29] D. B. Forrester, *op. cit.*, 127.

Thus, Monniatta, Mungah and Ummani became Ruth, Elizabeth and Ellen, respectively.

We must enquire as to what happened to the converts and their descendants, and what lasting contributions they made to the Christian presence in India in general, and to the Chengalpattu area in particular. Did they help in the breaking of caste distinctions, at least within the church, and what role did they play when the FCS was beginning to "harvest" Dalit converts in the rural areas? The Free Church congregation of 17 communicants was constituted in 1844 with the missionaries, their friends and the converts. In 1858 Rajahgopaul became the first pastor of the Native congregation (Anderson Church) of some 100 communicants including 60-70 native Christians. Even at this early stage of the native church, the caste origins of the Christians were evident in the Church and "having come from different Hindu communities they found it hard to form a homogeneous congregation."[30] This also resulted in considerable delay and difficulty in the selection of a successor to Rajahgopaul when he died in 1887.

Many of Anderson's converts found employment either in the schools run by the mission or with the government. A few such as Rajahgopaul and Venkataramiah were ordained as presbyters and made significant and lasting contributions to the Church in its early phase of growth. In 1870 Rajahgopaul established a Poor School[31] for Dalit children. This school, now in Royapuram, and the schools he founded for caste girls, are still functioning as Madras Diocesan schools. Rajahgopaul's poor school provided avenues of employment mostly as domestic servants and employees in shops; some of these students became teachers and Christian agents for missions.[32] However, no Dalit student of this school founded by the first and most famous convert of the Free Church, appears to have found a place in Miller's college next door.

[30] G. Pittendreigh and W. Meston, *op. cit.*, 70.

[31] *Madras Mission of the Church of Scotland: Centenary Booklet*, Madras: Diocesan Press, 1937, 22-25.

[32] A. Alexander, Rajahgopaul: *A Memorial Sketch*, Paisley, 1888, 23-24.

We have no record of the whereabouts of most of the descendants of most of these early generations of converts. However, a unique document[33] prepared by Pancharatnam and interviews with one of the distant descendants[34] reveal an interesting story of caste making a strong comeback among the descendants of the converts of the FCS. A new class of elite Christians, many of them educated at MCC, was evolving. They were active in the life of the Church and held influential positions in the secular world. These Christians of upper caste origins freely intermarried and caste was no boundary, with one glaring exception: practically none would marry a Dalit Christian! Loyalty to the caste-rejecting principles of the missions suddenly disappeared when it was time for a marriage. Upper caste Christians sought and married into families of upper caste Christians also of other missions, often among those who had moved from other districts to the Chennai and Chengalpattu areas. Although they were working in schools and churches in small and big towns among large numbers of Dalit Christians, the upper caste Christians would establish only limited civil relationships with them, never a marriage relationship, and there was clear segregation very early in the life of the Church. When the upper caste Christians moved away from small towns such as Chengalpattu, they ensured that their houses were sold only to Christians of upper caste origins! Pancharatnam's list as well as personal discussions with the descendants of upper caste converts reveal that most of them occupied high positions. A partial list would include: Administrative General of Madras, Chief Judge, other judges, pleaders, Port Officer, physicians and surgeons, Chief Medical Superintendent, Inspectors of Schools, Controller of Rents, Assistant Controller of Customs, and heads of educational

[33] Cullore Narayanaswamy Chetty was baptized by Braidwood on 28 August 1859. His son, J.N. Pancharatnam was requested by the Free Church missionary, Rev. W.S. Sutherland, to provide information on the early converts and their descendants. This short account (List of converts with a few short sketches, 1837-1880) is in File No. 84, United Theological College Archives.

[34] Interviews with Stephen Rajaratnam of Chengalpattu, December, 1994.

institutions. Needless to mention that the upper caste converts completely dominated the ecclesiastical and administrative positions in the Church and its institutions to the complete exclusion of any Dalit convert. There was power in English education; and there was more power if one were an upper caste Christian with English education at Madras Christian College.

FREE CHURCH INVESTS IN COLLEGE EDUCATION FOR THE ELITE

When William Miller arrived in 1862, Anderson's institution was not as popular as in the days of its founder. Anderson had achieved his major aims; he had converted young men and women, raised a native church and trained native teachers, preachers and missionaries to convey the good news to their fellow Indians. Miller, however, viewed the situation differently. He attributed the poor state of the school to "an error of policy" and a "premature attempt" on the part of the missions to take up evangelistic work.[35] Miller was not the right man to align with the Indian converts to continue the evangelistic work initiated by Anderson. Perhaps he disliked evangelism. Miller, however, was the right man among that peculiarly Scottish brand of missionaries who saw higher education as the means to the greater end of Christianizing India. Miller stuck to education and transformed Anderson's declining school into the leading centre of English higher education in South India. Miller's formidable energy and singular devotion, scholarship, innovations, personal wealth, charisma and influence helped the college acquire legendary status and prestige with the finest of buildings, library, hostels, magazine, literary associations, scholarships and prizes, a committed group of teachers and an annual enrollment of more than 600 eager students. Our concern here, however, is not the history of the college and its development; these can be found elsewhere.[36] We must assess the impact of the policies followed

[35] W. Miller, "Historical Sketch," xx-xxviii; *Short Account*, 14,15.

[36] See W. Miller, *Short Account;* A. Dayanandan, The Madras Christian College Timeline-150 Years. (1987). MCC Archives.

by Miller—for it was almost a one-man policy that shaped the college and influenced many other missionaries—on the Free Church and other missionary endeavours in Madras and Chengalpattu districts, especially in relation to the Dalit Christian community.

Miller was perhaps the strongest spokesperson for the brand of educational ministry the Scots such as Alexander Duff at Calcutta and John Wilson at Bombay were pursuing in India and were influencing other missions to pursue.[37] In order to convince fellow missionaries and the Church in Scotland, and to justify the disproportionate use of resources in running colleges, new ideas were evolved and forcefully argued and pursued. Thus, diffusion of Christian principles in a college was *preparatio evangelica*, a process of ploughing and sowing so that reaping could follow some time in the future. With the harvest of the upper castes there would be a downward filtration effect as Christianity trickled down to all the lower castes and therefore to the whole of India. Diffusion of Christian thought was a gradual process of leavening. Even if India did not become Christian, diffusion of Christian thought would lead to a sort of fulfilment where the Christian faith could be re-expressed in terms of Indian culture, and Christianity would fulfil the higher truths found in Hinduism.[38]

The first five years of Miller's work in India perhaps best reveals his aspirations, attitudes and prejudices. These are found in the two lectures he gave to home audiences on his furlough.[39] The mighty system of Hinduism, while venerable with grandeur and nobility of thought, yet was "an evil which the world should cease to be burdened with." The non-Hindus, i.e., the tribals and

---

[37] Ingleby has provided an excellent review and analysis of the ideological and philosophical background, the achievements, failures and influences and contemporary debate on the educational ministry of the Scottish missionaries. J. C. Ingleby, *Missionaries, Education and India: Issues in Protestant Missionary Education in the Long Nineteenth Century,* Delhi: ISPCK, 2000, Chapters 7-10.

[38] J. C. Ingleby, *op. cit.,* 261.

[39] W. Miller, *Two Lectures.*

Dalits, were "separate from true inhabitants," "mere adjuncts to the real people," and "as a gypsy is a stranger to a Scotsman." Miller thought nothing of the mass movements that had just begun among the Madigas in Telugu country or the conversion of Nadars that had already brought some thirty thousand people to Christianity in the South. These other missions had concentrated work on "aboriginal races," the "scattered and outlying sections of the people," and not "among the true people of the country," the "people who make up essential India."[40] Miller thought that "for three centuries and more Christianity had made no impression of any kind whatever upon the Hindus, that is the central, the dominating, mass among India's three hundred millions."[41] Therefore "as far as Hinduism and real Hindus were concerned the result was nothing."

Miller devoted all his energies towards the education of these "real Hindus," the upper caste youth. He noticed that as the Indians were beginning to adapt to the influence of British customs, languages, and laws the Hindus with "quick sighted shrewdness" found that Western English education "would soon become the main avenue to social distinction, to wealth and power."[42] So great was the desire for Western learning that the teaching of the scriptures "hindered not...scores and hundreds of the youth, belonging to the very central body of Hinduism, from flocking to them daily." Some of these students were so young, really children, but were filled with a desire for "prospective situations and hoped for salaries."[43]

Miller knew that the conversion of caste Hindus and Muslims caused more heat than light. Conversions were neither widespread nor making the significant social changes the founder Anderson had hoped for. There was "spasmodic action – violent heat and hurry and loud profession now, but by and by listless inactivity."[44] Miller was in no hurry to convert India. He was going "to prepare

---

[40] W. Miller, *Short Account*, 10.
[41] *Ibid.*, 10.
[42] W. Miller, *Two Lectures*, 22.
[43] *Ibid.*
[44] *Ibid.*, 52.

the way of the Lord, and make His paths straight."[45] The mission
should only do the preparatory work and "not seek to set up any
little native Church on a Scottish model in India at all."[46] In 1902
Miller baptized an old boy and his son "belonging to one of the
most prominent and respected Brahmin families," but this was a
rare event as he wrote, "I have not often taken a leading part in
baptizing any Hindu."[47] Thus, Miller was already clearly
eliminating, at least for that time, two of the three major aims with
which Anderson established the institution: those of conversion
and raising up of a native church. Referring to the direct evangelistic
work that the mission was carrying on in small towns and rural
areas, Miller found it incompatible with his mission since it had
no effect on the upper castes. "It appeals rather to those hitherto
beyond the sphere of English and of Christian thought." Since his
work was only preparatory, when would the harvest come and who
would do the harvesting? Miller was washing his hands of this
responsibility and delegating it to another agency, to be set up by
the Scottish mission, separate from the college, to work exclusively
among the leavened upper caste graduates of his college after they
left the institution. At least one man should devote himself to this
exclusively religious "agency for direct, systematic, simple Gospel
effort among those who have already, through our own
instrumentality, been brought somewhat under Gospel influence,
and fashioned somewhat in their character and thoughts on a
Christian model."[48]

We will refer to the success of the college later. What needs
to be emphasized here is not only that Miller's approach was entirely
elitist and biased against the lower castes, who in his opinion were
not the real people of the land, but also that he wanted mission
resources to be lavishly spent on his institution to educate the upper
castes. In this scheme of things, there was no place and no real
appreciation for the hundreds of missionaries working in rural fields

---

[45] *Ibid.*, 34.
[46] *Ibid.*, 43.
[47] Miller, *Short Account*, 22.
[48] W. Miller, *Two Lectures*.

among the poor, nor for the Dalits who became Christians in mass movements across the land, and certainly no concern for the education of Dalit youth in and around Chennai, including the Chengalpattu area. In 1907, when Adam Andrew was converting rural Dalits, the Free Church missionaries at the college thought it was still the time of sowing and the great harvest was yet to come.[49]

Duff and Miller and their approach to mission had many critics in many missions.[50] There was also widespread support for direct evangelistic work among the Dalits. Bishop Whitehead in Madras thought Duff's ideas were fallacious and argued for maintaining schools and colleges only for the education of Christians.[51] Duff's and Miller's methods had not worked out as anticipated; their approach was seen as a fundamental error; education had not done much yet for the great bulk of the 35 millions of the Madras Presidency; and many had started doubting the scriptural justification of their methods.[52] In 1887 the General Assembly of the Free Church expressed concern and sent a deputation to examine the Indian Scottish missions and decided to make a fundamental shift of resources into village evangelism. Fortunately the man who was to make this policy succeed and to raise up a native church among the Dalits had already arrived in India in 1879.

ADAM ANDREW AND DALIT CHRISTIANS

The Rev. Adam Andrew was sent as a FCS missionary to work in the rural areas. Andrew and his wife Elizabeth came to Chengalpattu in 1879. Before their arrival there had been only one European missionary at Chengalpattu, Rev. G. J. Metzger of the Basel

[49] G. Pittendrigh and W. Meston, *op. cit.*, 63.

[50] J.C. Ingleby, *op. cit.*, 336-375.

[51] G. Houghton, *op. cit.*, 15. For a perceptive analysis of the growing disenchantment with educational ministry and the shift towards support for village ministry and the controversy within the Free Church over the sharing of resources, see A. Porter, "Scottish Missions and Education in Nineteenth-Century India: The Changing face of 'Trusteeship'," *Journal of Imperial and Commonwealth History*, Vol. XVI (May 1988), 35-57.

[52] *Ibid.*

Mission as an agent of the Free Church. Between 1864 and 1871 he looked after the school and evangelized in the district assisted by mission converts, Appavu and Zynool Abideen. However, when Andrew arrived there were only about 20 Christians connected with the Free Church Mission in the Chengalpattu district. Some were Christian teachers employed by the mission; others were mission converts and their children. They were associated with the Chengalpattu and Kanchipuram schools and were members of the Esplanade Church in Madras under the pastoral care of Rev. Rajahgopaul, the first convert of John Anderson. In 1883 the Chengalpattu congregation was officially separated from the Esplanade Church and became a separate pastorate with Andrew as the first pastor.[53] Within ten years of his arrival Andrew, a foreign missionary, could achieve what the native agency of Anderson's Indian converts could not the previous thirty years. *The Madras Native Herald*, a journal founded by Anderson, has detailed reports of the extensive preaching tours of Rev. Rajahgopaul and fellow converts. By 1859 the native church consisted of 3 native missionaries, 2 licensed preachers, 2 superintending teachers and 15 agents involved in evangelistic work.[54] The Indian Christians of the Free Church visited hundreds of villages around Chennai and distant Thirupatore. They preached to all castes and outcastes and held spirited discussions, but with no obvious results in terms of conversion to Christianity from either the upper castes or the Dalits. The reasons for their failure to obtain converts need further study. There simply was no downward percolation.

Immediately after his arrival Andrew took charge of the Chengalpattu school and the small congregation. With the Chengalpattu town as his headquarters, he took the gospel to the neighbouring villages. In 1883 he set in motion organized evangelistic work with several catechists personally trained by him. Training local catechists was very important since at this stage he was dependent on other missions for the supply of preachers and

---

[53] Anne & P. Dayanandan, "One hundred years of St. Andrew's Church, Chengalpattu - 1893-1993," *St. Andrew's Centenary Souvenir*, 1993.
[54] *The Madras Native Herald*, Vol. XVIII (July 1859), 49-52.

only got "their worst men."[55] Together they launched into formidable village evangelism to caste Hindus as well as to Dalits. Andrew was not targeting the Dalits. In fact, he was careful not to offend the sensibilities of the villagers; he would first preach in the Brahmin section, then proceed to the Sudra area and finally to the *paracherry* where the Dalits lived.[56] The annual reports reveal the intensity of their evangelistic efforts. In 1880 two agents delivered 440 addresses to approximately 15,000 people. In 1884 over 2,000 villages were visited. In 1885 eight workers visited 2,290 villages preaching 4,049 times to 148,757 villagers. In 1888 some 5,340 addresses were given to an estimated 177,000 persons. 1542 visits were made to Hindu houses, and 25,000 tracts and handbills and 1,699 Bibles and Bible portions were sold. Schools were started as early as 1881 in five villages, ten years before any group movement was in sight, and by the time of the group conversions there were more than 20 schools and 650 students in these schools.

Andrew's baptismal record reveals that between 1880-1890 only 58 persons were baptized and 33 of these were children. Fifteen caste Hindus were baptized, nine of whom were Chettys. Only eight Paraiyar (Dalit) youth were baptized; all of them were likely to have been associated with the Christian families at Chengalpattu. About ten years after Andrew began his work, several leaders of Paraiyar villages requested him to establish schools for their children and teach them about Christ.[57] Andrew responded promptly to this unexpected movement from the outcaste quarters. It first happened in Narasamangalam, near Sriperumbudur. In 1889 the village leader, Mari, desired a school for the children of his village and expressed interest in Christianity. "After repeated visits to the Catechist, and learning more of Christian truth" on 27 May 1891 Mari at age 62 became a Christian, renamed Paul Mari, along with his wife and children.[58] The same day the families of Samuel

[55] A. Andrew in Report of the Madras Mission of the FCS (1885).

[56] A. Andrew, "Mission Work Done in A Moffusil District", *The Indian Evangelical Review*, 49 (July 1886), 1-13.

[57] *Madras Mission of the Church of Scotland: Centenary Booklet*; A. Andrew, "Chingleput Mission," *Madras Mission of the FCS, Report for 1891*, 9-12.

[58] *Madras Mission of the FCS, Report for 1891*, 9.

Annamalai and Luke Veeran were also baptized at Narasamangalam. Andrew erected a prayer-house and teachers' house at Narasamangalam, as he continued to do in all villages where Dalits were converting to Christianity. Paul Mari's decision influenced other relatives in the area and before the end of the year 15 converts from nearby Aranerry and 24 from Thathanoor were also baptized. This was the beginning of small group conversions that were spreading to distant villages around Kanchipuram and Chengalpattu. The next year about 240 people became Christians. Under the leadership of 60- year-old Paul, 33 people were baptized at Andreyapuram. The baptismal register kept by Andrew reveals that in each village the number of people converted varied between a few to a maximum of 55 at a time (Table 2).

Table 2

CONVERSION OF PARAIYAR IN CHENGALPATTU DISTRICT
(1891-1898)

Year	Village*	Number Baptized
1891	Narasamangalam	18
	Araneri	15
	Thathanur	24
1892	Walajabad	47
	Thathanur	37
	Pudhupedu	35
	Vedal	48
	Thandalam	17
	Andreyapuram	33
1893	Kutharambakkam	24
	Ariyambakkam	32
	Echur	17
1894	Andreyapuram	21
	Melrosapuram	55
1895	Athur	19
1896	Kayar	16
1897	Vallam	10
	Overtounpettai	19
1898	Kayar	15
	Melamaiyur	10

* Only those villages where more than 10 people were baptized are included in this Table

The Andreyapuram Christians originated from Perunthandalam, which was a typical village in the district with separate settlements for the caste and the Dalit people. Between 1892 and 1895 some 60 people settled at Konerikuppam on four acres of land granted by the Government.[59] In gratitude for Andrew's role the early settlers decided to call this first exclusively Christian settlement as Andreyapuram. In 1893 a number of families from Senkundram were settled on 72 acres of land at Melrosapuram. In 1896 another band of six families from Perunthandalam settled on 13 acres of land bought by Andrew with the help of money donated by Mr. Overtoun. After one year of sound training in Christian principles they were baptized on 31 December 1897 at Overtounpettai.[60] The group movement continued for many years.

The number of Christians rose rapidly from 20 to 1,491 during the fifteen years between 1879 and 1894. It was time for new pastorates to be established. In 1918 Andrew drew a detailed chart of the growth of the church in the district.[61] Thus, Kanchipuram became a separate pastorate in 1896. In 1898 Sriperumbudur and Melrosapuram were separated from Chengalpattu to become separate pastorates.

The early Christians had to endure persecution.[62] Those who had kept them in bondage now refused to give them jobs. They were ousted from the lands they had cultivated for a long time as sub-tenants. Lawsuits were brought to recover money supposedly due; false criminal charges were foisted; water was cut off from

[59] *FCS Report for 1892*, 14; A. Andrew's General Correspondence, Jan. 1894-July 1895, Letter to Tahsildhar, dated 10th Feb. 1894, No. 54, MCC Archives.

[60] G. Pittendrigh and W. Meston, *op. cit.*, 77-83; A. Andrew. "A Thirty Years' Retrospect", *In and Around Madras, Being a Report of the Work of the United Free Church of Scotland Mission for 1908-1909*, 4-8.

[61] UTC Archives, CHOS, File, 89,2; Anne & P. Dayanandan, op. cit. For the growth of the Christian community between 1900 and 1924, see *In and Around Madras, Madras Mission of the UFCS* (1924), 4.

[62] *FCS Report for 1892*, 14.

their rice fields; the thatched school buildings were set on fire; and people were beaten up while sleeping in their huts. Sites or houses for catechists were refused. Most early Christians stood firm and endured such persecution, and a few migrated away to other villages.

When Adam Andrew baptized 13 families at Melrosapuram on 3rd October 1894, the first among them was a 42 year-old woman, Sinnakolandai (literally, small child). She became Dayanithi. She was baptized along with her husband Jesudasan and five children. Two years earlier while visiting her relatives near Thathanoor she was impressed by the education the children were receiving in Christian schools.[63] She too desired to become a Christian and send her children to a school. It took her two years to convince her husband and other relatives in her village. Unfortunately the villagers today have no memory of this event; neither was it possible to trace the descendants of Sinnakolandai's children (Gnanamary, Nallammal, Asirvatham, Arputham and Bakkiam) who were baptized by Andrew.

It is difficult to comprehend the indefatigable energy and determination with which Adam Andrew must have worked to bring about transformation in the lives of his converts, and Paraiyar in general. He and Mrs. Andrew worked for 35 years in Chengalpattu. Rev. J. H. Maclean joined Andrew in 1895 and furthered the evangelistic and educational work around Kanchipuram and Sriperumbudur. Two years before Andrew left, there were 67 schools with 131 teachers and a total of 2,722 students of which 2,145 were Christian boys and girls.[64] The Kanchipuram station alone sold 100,000 Bibles and books that year (compared with a total sale of 241,270 for all 15 stations of the UFCS in Asia, Africa, New Hebrides and Jamaica).[65]

---

[63] "Notes from the Mission Field," *Free Church of Scotland Monthly* (December 1, 1894), 284.

[64] *United Free Church Report on Foreign Missions for 1913*, (Edinburgh, 1914).

[65] *Ibid.*

Andrew was at once a man of God, a fighter for the freedom of the oppressed, a keen student of social and economic realities, who always supported his conclusions with careful statistics, an agricultural and irrigation expert with a scientific bent of mind, and a fund-raiser and builder of institutions. He was constantly sharing his views both in missionary publications and in the popular press. His articles in the *Madras Mail* on such topics as education, irrigation, agriculture, cultivation, and extraction of fiber from plantain, and famine relief were published as two booklets.[66] The *Mail* in turn published a brief but good account of Andrew's achievements.[67] At Melrosapuram Andrew carried out pioneering experiments in well irrigation. He kept careful record of water levels and water requirements for agriculture and horticulture. The Government donated to him an oil engine and a pump as well as a large 16-foot Canadian wind engine and pump. Based on his experiments, the oil engine was widely used for irrigation in other parts of India. Melrosapuram was a thriving farm colony and a model for other such colonies elsewhere in India. At Overtounpettai Andrew excavated an irrigation tank in the typically ancient South Indian style, a tank that is still functional.[68] He also established co-operative banks in nearly all the Christian villages where non-Christians too, became members of the society.[69]

Within four years of his arrival in India and well before the group movement started, Andrew became aware of the oppressed situation of the outcastes, and submitted a paper in 1883 to the Sub-Collector of Chengalpattu.[70] When no response was forthcoming he appealed to the Director of Public Instruction. He was convinced that there was "little that they themselves, if unassisted, can do" and pleaded for the beginning of "a new educational era for the Pariah population by giving an enhanced

[66] A. Andrew, *Indian Problems*, Madras, 1905; *New Movement*, Madras, 1907.
[67] "The Rev. A. Andrew," *Madras Mail*, 19th October, 1909.
[68] *In and Around Madras, Report for 1924*, 28.
[69] *Ibid*.
[70] *Madras Mail*, 19th October, 1909, 2.

grant for all who are willing to do something for them in raising them up, and making them better and more intelligent subjects."[71] He wanted a more liberal scale of grants as was then enjoyed by certain tribal groups under the scheme of the Grants-in-Aid Code. This was not an act of charity or chivalry, but a true expression of Christian solidarity with the oppressed and was unconnected to any motive of winning them over to Christianity. Andrew took the matter to the Government in Madras and the Parliament in England. The Government Order of 1893, hailed as the Panchama Magna Charta, provided for grants-in-aid for the education of Paraiyar students and the supply of land to outcastes for cultivation and settlement.[72] This is how the so-called Panchama lands came into existence in many parts of the Madras Presidency. Andrew was proud to be known as the "Pariah Andrew."[73]

The Andreyapuram-Overtounpettai complex offers interesting opportunities for an understanding of the progress made by Dalit Christians in this area. The Dalits in the parent village, Perunthandalam, are non-Christians. Both Andreyapuram and Overtounpettai defy definition as villages. They were established as settlements of people detached from the parent village. Yet the parent village with many relatives, rituals and cultural practices was just a stone's throw away. We have already lost valuable information as to how these small communities interacted with their non-Christian relatives, resisted former practices that were part of their lives, and kept their Christian faith.

Why did the Dalits of Chengalpattu area convert to Christianity? The early events leading to conversion of their ancestors are now lost in the memory of most Dalit Christians. Yet, some of the older Christians, especially the retired teacher-catechists, recall their parents and elders telling them why their ancestors converted to Christianity. The account below is based on what my father and

[71] *Ibid.*

[72] For details see G. Houghton, *op. cit.*, 99-122; S. Anandhi, *Land to the Dalits: Panchami Land Struggle in Tamil Nadu*, Bangalore: Indian Social Institute, 2000.

[73] *Madras Mail, loc. cit.*

two of his uncles (converted by the Rev. Maclean, a colleague of Adam Andrew) recounted on many occasions. Poor and oppressed as they were, each small Paraiyar community had leaders who could comprehend what Christianity offered. They saw in Christ a God who cared for them; a good and innocent man tortured and killed. They heard that Christ was against all forms of oppression and stood by the poor. They were equally fascinated with the Old Testament characters, and while converting, were proud to adopt new names such as Abraham, Moses, David and Ruth. The missionaries appeared to them as sincere people who sat with them and even ate with them simple ragi gruel made in their houses. They also conversed with them in Tamil and sympathized with their woes. They were particularly impressed by the potential of Christian education which the missionaries were offering their children to free themselves from the chain of ignorance, to taste freedom, and to lead the kind of dignified life that they and their ancestors had not been permitted to live. Perhaps their children would someday rise up in social status and occupy positions which they themselves could not even dream of. The missionaries and catechists were now inundating their lives with songs and stories, prayers and new concepts. In a matter of weeks and months they could see for the first time in history their young boys and girls sing, recite verses and pray, and, above all, read. Even though the first converts could not read, it was extraordinarily gratifying for them to see that their children and grandchildren could read. They were no more without a book; they were now people of a book, a sacred book.

Most major mass movements to Christianity in the Punjab, the Telugu country, and in Southern India were initiated by individual Dalit leaders.[74] The small group conversions in north Tamil Nadu under the influence of the FCS (as well as the established CS and the MMS) were not associated with any one leader. Each village seemed to have had its own leader whose influence extended to no more than their relatives in the village or perhaps in a few neighbouring villages. These villages, from the east coast to the

[74] John C. B. Webster, *op. cit.*, 39-52.

interior regions around Arakkonam, had no common leaders or platforms; it is therefore a mystery that there was this great climate of conversion and Dalit leaders from a very wide region would respond almost identically to three different missions. Perhaps the villagers learnt through word of mouth at work in rice fields and while shopping or through marriage alliances of the goodness of this new religion. There is no record of the conversion of any entire village. There were occasional minor conflicts among the converts and their non-convert relatives in the same village. Yet it would soon resolve itself into a situation of "live and let live." Dalits were free to convert, move out to a new settlement or to a new section of the village, or continue to live in their old houses, but now professing a new religion.

EDUCATION OF DALIT CHRISTIANS: NOT IN THE MILLER TRADITION

A major recurring theme during Andrew's time was the desire for schools in Paraiyar villages. Andrew often responded by asking the villagers to help build a thatched roof classroom so he could provide a teacher and the necessary supervision. As early as 1893 at the early stage of the group movements, Andrew was supervising 22 village schools with 656 students. For the descendants of most converts education was not available beyond the primary school level, and certainly not beyond the high school level. Yet education was the single most important avenue of progress available for the converts. Here we examine how higher education was not made available to the Dalits in a college established by the FCS.

Rev. Duncan Forrester was the last of the educational missionaries to come to the Madras Christian College from the Church of Scotland.[75] The Scots, according to Forrester, came to India with the conviction that learning, true godliness and the equality of men are inseparable; they saw value in education only when it is turned relentlessly against caste, and "the Scots were the first to use education explicitly as an invaluable weapon in the

[75] D. B. Forrester, *op, cit.*, 28.

struggle against caste and to affirm that a liberal Christian education could not recognize or tolerate caste observances within its walls."[76] This clearly was not what really happened when they came to India. Anderson and Miller might have had much to preach and write against caste, undoubtedly with conviction. However, in practice they were in fact strengthening the institution of caste. A liberal education at Madras Christian College was not made available to the Dalit converts of their own mission. The college was for the elite because the attitude of most of the Free Church educational missionaries was elitist. This strongly contrasts with recent studies of Balasundaram[77] in connection with the work of London Mission Society among Dalits. Those missionaries came ideologically and theologically predisposed to work among Dalits and provide them liberty, equality, and every means of social elevation.

Miller and his colleagues were quite unsympathetic to the efforts of their fellow Free Church missionary, Adam Andrew. The Notes and Extracts column of the MCC Magazine carried editorial comments on reports of various missions. Andrew's account of village evangelistic work in the 1889 Report of the Madras Mission of the Free Church was reviewed with callous sarcasm by the editor of the magazine. Andrew's characteristically meticulous statistical report was considered suspect by the editor who ventured to offer uncalled for advice. "We hold that such statistics are utterly worthless as a measure of work done." The evangelistic agents' "duty as preachers and teachers of the Gospel of Jesus Christ is...to make the people free."[78] In the ensuing years the magazine continued to comment on the mission reports from elsewhere, even rejoicing in the conversions reported by the Santal Mission of the Free Church or the Mysore Mission of the Wesleyan Methodists.[79] However, there was neither rejoicing nor applauding, not a word

---

[76] *Ibid.*

[77] Franklyn J. Balasundaram, *Dalits and Christian Mission in the Tamil Country*, Bangalore: Asian Trading Corporation, 1997, 56-80.

[78] "Notes and Extracts," *MCC Magazine*, Vol. 7 (1889-90), 943.

[79] "Notes and Extracts," *MCC Magazine*, Vol. 11 (1893-94), 624-5, 690, 754-5.

on the Free Church's most significant period in history, the group movements of 1891 and the following years, nor of Andrew's pioneering role in the "Panchama Magna Charta." Andrew's achievements must have been too close for comfort and threatening to the assumptions of the educational missionary professors at MCC. Miller and Andrew were poles apart. The difficulties faced by Andrew in the sharing of resources within the local Madras Mission Council of the Free Church led to his bitter complaint to Edinburgh.[80]

As we have seen, the group conversions that originated in Narasamangalam in 1891 were reaching a high mark by 1895. Miller, as the Moderator of the General Assembly of the Free Church of Scotland in 1896, made his views on the conversion of Dalits known to his home audience.

> Yet the impression has got abroad that those who are thus gathering to Christ's standard are in the full evangelical sense converted men, in short that we have in India a repetition not of Moses and the Exodus, but of Peter and the day of Pentecost. And no very strenuous effort to correct the false impression is made by those who lead the movement.[81]

This was Miller's typical stubborn way of both justifying his own work that was constantly under criticism, and refusing to accept the effect of the good news on people who have not had the benefit of education that a college like MCC could offer. In the same address Miller suggested that largely through the efforts of Christian education such as his own the most thoughtful of India's sons were beginning to ask, "What must I do to be saved." Such an elitist attitude was common among others who shared Miller's views on missionary education. T. E. Slater of the L.M.S. would not give sufficient credit to the power of gospel, as he thought that preaching touched "the mind of any nation only at the point of its weakest

---

[80] A. Porter, *op. cit.*, 74.

[81] W. Miller, "The Bearing of Mission Work on the Life of the Church" [Opening Address to the General Assembly of the Free Church of Scotland 1896] *MCC Magazine* (July 1896).

and most ignorant individuals."[82] The Government Superintendent of Census was more sympathetic:

> It is neither good Christianity nor good sense to offer the Paraiyan the arid stone of theological speculation, while he lacks the bread of humanity...The hope of a decent life on earth is not any more or any less a bribe than the hope of a blissful eternity hereafter.[83]

Andrew, who knew the Paraiyar better than any other Free Church missionary believed,

> Their motives may be mixed, they may desire education for their children, and expect some help in the day of trouble, and seek a better social status; but along with these there is a belief that Christianity is the true religion, and that embracing it means the bettering their condition in this world and in the world to come.[84]

Christianity came to the Dalits because long ago on a mountain in Israel the Kingdom of God was promised to those who were humble, persecuted, hated, rejected, insulted and declared evil. After years of oppression the Dalits "were worried and helpless, like sheep without a shepherd"[85] and Andrew and Goudie were a few among the many who were needed and willing to gather the sheep. The Dalits listened for years before they moved. They discussed the claims of Christianity with their family and friends and in their village councils. After weeks of hesitation and fear, one day they might decide to approach an evangelist and ask him to teach them about Christ.

> Then after many days or weeks or months it may be, they decide to send a petition to the missionary asking him to receive them as Christians and to send a teacher to their village to live among them and teach their children.[86]

---

[82] Cited in J. C. Ingleby, *op. cit.*, 265.

[83] "Preaching the Kingdom: Village Mass Movements", *In and Around Madras, Being a Report of the Work of the UFCSM for 1911-1912*, 10

[84] A. Andrew, *Madras Mission of the Free Church of Scotland Report for 1892*, 15.

[85] Mathew 9: 36.

[86] "Preaching the Kingdom; Village Mass Movements,", 10.

The kingdom of God was here and now for the Dalits, and the tongues of fire did spread out and touch them. Are not all conversions spiritual, "a mysterious work of the Spirit?"[87] The limitations to their material progress came from Miller and his colleagues who denied them avenues of advancement through higher education.

It is worth remembering, as pointed out by Houghton,[88] that most missionaries were happy that the Church was taking roots among the Dalits. The Brahmins and the upper castes have had their chance and rejected it, and the missions were "compelled by force of circumstances, rather than led by any deliberate design, to turn to the Pariah."[89] Good news to the oppressed did bring liberation here and now and the Dalits had a right to cling to it. The good news was simple and made abundant sense to hundreds of illiterate converts who in turn chose to bring it to their fellow men and women. In every Dalit Christian village the leaders walked in day and at night, with a stick in hand and a lantern held high, in blistering heat and rain, to pray and tell stories and sing songs so that others could hear the story of Jesus who was now filling their lives with a newfound joy and hope.

It was clear to Miller and his colleagues that only the elite upper castes should be the recipients of the undoubtedly superior English education that was offered at the Madras Christian College. The first hostel that Miller built in 1885, the Students' Home, was exclusively for his Brahmin students. Soon there was another hostel for Brahmin students (chiefly, Vaishnavas), and yet another for non-Brahmin Hindus, and a separate one for Indian Christians. Such exclusivity was to change only in the mid-1920s. Some ten years after Miller had left, the total strength of students at MCC was

[87] L. Newbigin, *The Gospel in a Pluralist Society*, Geneva: WCC, 1989, 182.

[88] G. Houghton, *op. cit.* 100.

[89] These are the words of Henry Whitehead, Bishop of Madras, in *Report of the Fourth Decennial Missionary Conference held in Madras December 11th-18th, 1902*, London: Christian Literature Society, 1903, 9.

854.[90] Of these 48.5% were Brahmins, 22% non-Brahmin Hindus and 23% were Indian Christians. The 200 Indian Christians did not include any Dalit Christians from the neighbourhood either of the Free Church or of the Church of Scotland and MMS, societies that were cooperating and contributing to run the college.

For the upper caste Hindus and many Muslims MCC offered all they could hope for: the best English education under outstanding teachers; the best infrastructure facilities, hostel facilities, co-curricular activities and opportunities for self-governance and personality development; immediate employment opportunities in a wide variety of professions; a benevolent Miller who would help provide for all these; as well as an atmosphere of religious freedom where conversion to Christianity was not on the agenda. The 1917-18 College Calendar listed 4207 students who had graduated from the college. Details of employment were not shown for 677 graduates, but the remaining 3530 occupied every enviable position of employment then available. A similar situation was reported by Studdert-Kennedy who found that of the 2,920 graduates out of a total of 4500 graduates listed in the 1921 Calendar, 43% were government servants, 31% lawyers, 22% school or college teachers and the rest engineers, doctors, businessmen and churchmen.[91] Studdert-Kennedy also found 139 MCC alumni listed in the early 1930s publication, "Who's Who in Madras", in prominent positions, many active simultaneously in different positions or moved freely from one to another. Between 1920-1930 six MCC alumni were Ministers, including two Chief Ministers.[92] This tradition continued even after Miller left in 1907, and MCC graduates occupied every important niche of influence and opportunity for their caste and community as well as political and ideological groups to progress. The Dalits were obviously not a part of this influential elite. Christians of upper caste too benefited from this education. K.T.Paul, Chenchhia, Chakkarai and others would not only occupy

[90] MCC Calendar, Part A, 1920-21.
[91] G. Studdert-Kennedy, *Providence and the Raj: Imperial Mission and Missionary Imperialism*, London: Sage Publication, 1998.
[92] *Ibid.*

good positions but also debate on the nature and future of the Indian church. Even at this stage the church was predominantly Dalit in numbers. Yet Dalit Christians had no education, and hence lacked the social standing necessary to participate in negotiations or develop theologies relevant for the emerging church.

The Anderson School at Kanchipuram and the St. Columba's School at Chengalpattu were established by Anderson as feeder schools to supply upper caste students to the Central Institution, and less than a handful of boys and girls did convert to Christianity. Andrew took charge of these schools in 1879. The schools were potentially a good avenue towards college education for the rural Dalit Christian youth. As early as 1893 Andrew had established a boys' boarding home at Chengalpattu, and in 1895 a girls' boarding home for providing advanced education for the children of rural Dalit converts. But college education was closed to them because MCC was stubbornly wedded to the "downward percolation" theory, and had no use for the young Paraiyar. Rajahgopual too, as we have seen, established a school as early as 1870 in the Big Paracherry in Madras for Dalit students. These students too found no favour with Miller. Rev. Leslie Newbigin was a Free Church (UFCS) missionary at Kanchipuram between 1936 and 1946. In his autobiography, Bishop Newbigin was emphatic.

> In spite of the fact that the Church of Scotland was the parent mission of the Madras Christian College – the most prestigious educational institution in the whole of India – not one single boy from the villages of the Kanchipuram area had been sent to the college. They were judged unfit.[93]

Newbigin also commented upon this sad state of affairs on another occasion.

> I speak here with rather vivid memories. At the time of the Tambaram Conference I was a district missionary 25 miles from here. Not a single product of those village congregations had ever been admitted to the Madras Christian College. It was not in the Miller tradition. I made it my business to batter at these

---

[93] L. Newbigin, *Unfinished Agenda: An Autobiography*, London: SPCK, 1985, 59-60.

doors until a few young men from these villages were admitted. They are now playing their part in the life of the Church in Madras.[94]

Miller was not only a FCS missionary but also the Chairman for a period of the Madras FCS Presbytery. Yet a major source of emancipation and rapid progress, namely education at MCC, would not be available to the Dalit Christians of the Free Church of Scotland Mission, or to the Dalit children of the Established Church of Scotland in the Arakkonam area, or to the MMS Christians of Thiruvallur and associated villages. Was not the Madras metropolis large enough to support other Christian colleges where converts of these other missions might have found a place? Here again Miller and MCC had preempted the option of any other viable Protestant Christian college in this area. As we have seen earlier, Miller's plan to upgrade the Free Church Institution into a central college for southern India was heartily endorsed by seven different missionary bodies then operating in Madras, and the Methodist Missionary Society as well as the Church Missionary Society were already making financial contributions in 1877 when the institution became Madras Christian College. In 1913 the London Missionary Society, the American Baptist Foreign Missionary Society, and the American Arcot Mission also joined MCC as contributing bodies. These developments did strengthen MCC and added to its pre-eminence, but just as surely they forestalled the emergence of any other Protestant college where Dalit Christians might have had access to a good college education in Madras. After the Disruption

---

[94] L. Newbigin, "The Spiritual Foundations of our Work," *The Christian College and National Development: ISS-FERES Consultation of Principals of Christian College, Tambaram*, Madras: Christian Literature Society, 1967, 234. The International Missionary Council was held at Tambaram in 1938. The college now does offer an education to Christians, and up to fifty per cent of its enrolment is Christian, including Dalit Christians. The reason for this has more to do with the government's educational policies of reservation for minorities since Independence than to any conscious effort on the part of the college to promote the education of Dalits.

the Established Church of Scotland did start its own school in Black Town, close to the Free Church institution. This was raised to a second-grade college in 1887, only to be closed and merged with MCC in 1911. Unfortunately, the Free Church institution was its model and therefore it did not provide college education to Dalit Christians during its independent existence.

All that the Dalit Christian youth could hope for was education that terminated either at the primary or 8th standard or in rare instances high school levels. Teachers and preachers within the Dalit Christian community could be trained and become leaders only with this level of education. Village Christians were often angry with the missionaries who followed after Andrew because the missionaries would not recommend their children for college or professional education. It was likely that some missionaries working in the rural areas did get used to the idea that the Dalit Christians need or deserve no more than school education. More often, they were helpless because they had no college to which to send even the brightest youngsters, even if they wanted to. Such discrimination was to continue even after MCC moved from the city in 1937 into the spacious Tambaram campus. Several Dalit Christians from the rural congregations found employment at the college as construction workers, gardeners, watchmen, attendees, servants and cooks. Many were accommodated as a separate class in a "Model Village" adjoining the college. Their children and grandchildren found themselves in similar jobs at the college and none were enabled to study and sit alongside as a professor in the college. It is quite obvious that Miller was not talking about the Dalit Christians of his own Mission in the very district where he was running his famous college when he said that the Christian community had grown "in social position, in education, in wealth, in general character, and similar elements of weight and influence."[95]

The general aims of missionary education were the conversion of pupils; providing knowledge of the Bible; the creation of leaders

---

[95] W. Miller, "An Address", *Harvest Field* (February 1900), 46.

as pastors, evangelists and teacher-catechists; and development of the Christian community, including the general social amelioration of the poor people among them. These aims were "powerfully subverted by the Scots"[96] by their own brand of an elitist aim of *preparatio evangelica*. More than a hundred years were wasted in clinging to this theory and propping it up with concepts such as diffusion, fulfilment and downward percolation. This had disastrous consequences for the Dalit Christians in particular and Dalits in general, as well as for the cause of Christianity in India. Their colleges did not provide higher education for Dalits; instead they helped those who opposed their progress with the powerful weapon of English education, promoting upper caste hegemony. As the Lindsay Commission put it, "They provided a body of men who are influential in Government service, at the Bar, in trade, commerce, and in politics, but not leaders of the Church."[97] The Lindsay Commission also found that in the thirty-eight colleges it visited there had been only about a dozen conversions over a ten-year period.[98] When Christianity did come to the rural areas of Chengalpattu district it was not through conversion of the children in the schools, but through group movement of people of all ages. Local leaders and teacher-catechists had to settle with no more than a high school education. The untiring efforts of men like Andrew and Goudie could not match the requirements of a vast number of poverty-stricken villages, and the social development of the Christian community has been painfully slow, constant struggle against forces of oppression that still haunt them in subtle ways, even within the Church. As the Lindsay Commission noted,

> The fact remains that at the top, in the Christian colleges, we are teaching non-Christians and the sons and daughters of Christian preachers and laymen from the towns and cities, while Christian

[96] J. C. Ingleby, *Missionaries, Education and India*, 374.

[97] *The Christian College in India: The Report of the Commission on Christian Higher Education in India*, London: Oxford University Press, 1931.

[98] *Ibid.*, 107-108.

boys and girls from the villages, coming out of the mass
movement areas, are rarely to be found."[99]

At MCC there was none to be found. As Ingleby put it, "amongst
many missionaries education had now become an end in itself. It
was a good thing to offer – as a sort of social duty, and it provided
people with 'social uplift' or if they were already amongst the
privileged classes, with a better life."[100] The Dalit Christians of
Chengalpattu area were obviously not a privileged class; and it
was not in Miller's tradition to socially uplift the Dalits. As English
higher education was not offered equally to every strata of society
it did not break down traditional hierarchies. Also, "the very elitism
of the system especially in higher education, could not but make
the educated Indian feel as patronizingly towards the illiterate
masses, as the colonial sahibs felt towards him."[101] Forty-four years
of efforts at MCC added no significant number of converts to the
local church during Miller's time; neither did it a century later.
The denial of higher education to Dalits and Dalit Christians in a
missionary institution was unChristian. It also hindered the rapid
progress of the Church that was emerging in the rural areas by
failing to provide Dalit Christians as church leaders and individuals
in positions of influence. Those who benefited from the educational
policies of Anderson, Miller and others surely adored the
missionaries. And in post-British India the same elite would further
disadvantage the Dalit Christians and the Church by influencing
government policies. What trickled down was the power of
education to strengthen caste and class-consciousness, as well as
to consolidate caste hegemony over the Dalits both in the secular
world and within the Church, by denying them opportunities for
progress.

---

[99] *Ibid.*, 60.

[100] J. C. Ingleby, *Missionaries, Education and India*, 369.

[101] R. C. Heredia, "Education and Mission, Schools as Agent of
Evangelisation," *Economic and Political Weekly* (September 16, 1995)
2338.

COMMENTS ON CONVERSION AND LIFE OF DALIT CHRISTIANS

In this final section I summarize my own impressions based on discussion, personal observation, and experience on the role played by missionaries, the reasons why the Dalits responded to them both in the Free Church and other neighbouring fields, and the life and progress of the early converts. For the Dalits of northern Tamil Nadu, so close to Chennai, the Good News took a surprisingly long time to stir souls. It was not presented to the people with any seriousness until rather late in the nineteenth century. It was the Chengalpattu and Kanchipuram schools that Anderson started, and not his central institution, that some forty years later brought Andrew to these towns and helped him reach out to the villages. The Disruption of the Church of Scotland was a blessing in disguise for the Dalits. It took Christianity to the Arakkonam-Sholinghur area. Together Andrew, other Free Church missionaries, and missionaries of the Established Church helped the Dalit Christians lay a strong foundation for the Church in Northern Tamil Nadu. Although Anderson also had a preferential option for the upper caste youth, the institutions he founded later offered education to the children of Dalit converts. For example, Anderson converted five caste girls aged 11 and 12 —spiritual conversion or not—and because of them a boarding school took shape and exists today as the Northwick school. Andrew and others sent many rural Dalit Christian girls for high school education to Northwick. The St. Columba's, Anderson and Goudie schools are testimonies to Anderson's lasting contributions. Andrew was able to build on these, and establish numerous schools for boys and girls in this area.

The first convert at Andreyapuram was Paul. Paul's son, Sundararaj Paul became a headmaster of the American College High School at Madurai. Some became teachers, some nurses, and one a driver. Others continued to work on their own, and mostly in other people's rice fields. However, this and other villages cannot boast of judges, doctors, engineers, high administrative or police officers, professors, artists, bankers, politicians or business people.

About a hundred years after the establishment of Overtounpettai, a descendant from this settlement, Azariah, son of Masilamony, and educated at MCC, became the Bishop in Madras.

Several factors conspired to slow down the emancipating potential of conversion with serious consequences for the progress of the converts and their descendants. The true dimensions of the forces that had enslaved them were not revealed to them. Most missionaries were aware of these factors and some such as Andrew and Goudie were willing to fight for the rights of Dalit Christians. However, the Dalit converts were not educated to comprehend the forces that kept them suppressed, let alone inspired to organize and fight for their rights. The early converts too did everything in their capacity to suppress the facts of their origins from their children, to spare them of this painful past. There was to be no festival to mark this historic moment of their conversion, no Moses to constantly remind them of their past. Instead, this first step of liberation gave them a false sense of superiority within their small world. All that they had for comparison was the less desirable world of their unconverted relatives and friends. They were to have no more social intercourse with them, and for good reasons of keeping their faith and avoiding apostasy. In this process any possibility of solidarity with the Dalits at large was sacrificed. The stronger force of oppression already present within the Church, and about to intensify as caste discrimination among the Christians was unknown and unrevealed to the early Dalit Christians. In their innocence they believed what the non-Dalit preachers proclaimed: there was no caste within Christianity. Dalit Christians took seriously what Christianity taught them— love, kindness, forgiveness, sharing and brotherhood—and deeply trusted all Christians, missionaries or Indians. The descendants had to learn the hard way, in every generation, that the brotherhood their ancestors were promised did not exist in their Church.

Throughout northern Tamil Nadu the Dalit Christians lived in islands and in ignorance of the true dimensions of the forces of oppression. There were neither leaders nor a climate that would permit the emergence of leaders who could promote the progress of the Dalit community. The missionaries, pastors, teacher-catechists and village elders were the only leaders, but they operated in a hierarchy that mostly dealt with things spiritual. There were grand annual gatherings for harvest festivals, but these occasions were never used for any form of education of the social realities of the converts. Dr. Ambedkar, in his insightful analysis of the condition of the converts, found the Dalit Christians "leaderless and therefore unable to mobilize for the redress of their wrongs."[102] Ambedkar also felt that, from a sociological point of view, the doctrine of original sin was fraught with disaster. "When he was a Hindu his fall was due to his Karma. When he becomes a Christian he learns that his fall is due to the sins of his ancestor." For Ambedkar the consequence was that the "untouchable convert instead of being energized to conquer his environment contents himself with the belief that there is no use in struggling." Certainly sin was a dominant theme in the early days of evangelism, whether it was Anderson addressing the young upper caste students or missionaries confronting the rural Dalits.

We have made reference to the neighbouring areas/districts and other missions that worked among Dalits of North Tamil Nadu. Although the focus here has been on Chengalpattu area and the FCS, brief mention should be made of the contemporary role of other missions in order to appreciate the response of the Dalit people. All were Paraiyar and in identical social and economic conditions. In Madras City the Established Church of Scotland (CS) started a school after the Disruption, just five minutes walk away from the FCS school in Black Town.[103] This school and the girls' school started in 1847 were also intended to educate caste students. In 1869, of the 523 students 393 were caste Hindus, 104 were Muslims, 18 were Christians and 8 were East Indians; there were no Dalit students in the school. The involvement of the Church of

---

[102] B. R. Ambedkar, *Collected Research Articles on "Christianizing the Untouchables,"* Madras: Dalit Liberation Education Trust, 1994, 74-81.

[103] See Beth Walpole, The Church of Scotland Mission: Archival Material, 1796-1912 (1997), UTC Archives.

Scotland with Dalits began only after 1867 when the mission expanded its field of work to Arakkonam. Many years of evangelism and educational work in the villages, especially under the leadership of Rev. Henry Rice, brought Dalits to Christianity. Group movements occurred frequently after 1893 in Puthur, Kilpaukkam, Aiyaneri and other places near Arakkonam and Sholinghur.[104] In 1898 Rice founded a peasant settlement at Essanur on 22 acres of land provided by the Government. In 1885 there were only 43 Christians and 4 schools. When Rice retired in 1911 after 26 years in Arakkonam, the area had 8 outstation congregations, 595 Christians, 12 schools, 9 catechists, 21 Christians and 10 non-Christian teachers.[105]

The areas evangelized by the MMS lie sandwiched between the fields of the Free Church and the CS. Ten years before Narasamangalam, and the year Andrew arrived, MMS already had three congregations at Ikkadu, Kandigai and Otthikkadu with 54, 39 and 59 Christians respectively as a result of the evangelistic work of William Burgess. George M. Cobban who followed him established additional village congregations. Initially Cobban was strongly prejudiced in favour of Brahmins, but the unjust relationships he saw changed his sympathies and he thought of the social and religious elevation of the outcastes as the noblest work he could be engaged in.[106] From 1888 onwards William Goudie carried on work among Dalits in a manner remarkably similar to that of Adam Andrew.[107] "Pariah Andrew" of FCS, and Goudie of MMS who saw "Christ in a Pariah" and was therefore enabled to see the "Pariah in Christ," [108] and Henry Rice, "the maker and

---

[104] A copy of the baptismal register of the St. Andrew's Church, Arakkonam (1880-1925) is in the Archives of UTC (Book No. 5).

[105] B. Walpole, *op. cit.*

[106] G. M. Cobban, "Village work in the Madras District", *The Harvest Field* (Nov., 1882), 140.

[107] W. Goudie, "The Pariahs and the Land", *The Harvest Field* (July 1894), 490-500; W. Goudie, "Social work among the Pariahs", *The Indian Evangelical Review* (April 1893), 314; J. Lewis, *William Goudie*, London: Wesleyan Methodist Missionary Society, 1923.

[108] J. Lewis. *William Goudie*, 118.

builder" of the CS together were indomitable men who helped change the life of many Dalits in northern Tamil Nadu.

The life and progress of the early Dalit Christians of these three regions evangelized by the three missions appear to be quite similar to each other. After conversion education in mission schools became the only viable means of progress for the descendants of the converts. Education helped them find jobs in mission schools and hospitals and in lower levels in government offices, and in private concerns. Since college education was denied to them they could not obtain highly paid or top level jobs, and even in the Christian institutions where they worked the administration was in control of upper caste Christians. In the new settlements limited land of a few cents to acres was available for some to farm as tenants of the mission. However, land was not a route to prosperity for the Dalit Christians. Andrew did establish at Melrosapuram a centre that offered training in agriculture, horticulture and other skills such as weaving and bee keeping. However, the students trained there had no land, money, entrepreneurial skills, or connections to pursue these avenues of progress to make significant changes in their economic condition. Mrs. Andrew started a lace-making school[109] at the Chengalpattu girls' boarding school to train village girls to earn supplemental income, but this too could never become an industry that could transform the economic life of the Dalit Christians. The small Dalit Christian villages, usually not more than about fifty families, did not provide for the development of high schools or technical institutes. All these factors, combined with the migration of the educated youth to the towns and cities have had an adverse effect on the development of these villages. Most of the villages associated with the Free Church now appear less cared for, and show no progress befitting one hundred years of existence.

Why did the Dalits convert to Christianity? Some knowledge of the religious and cultural world of the Paraiyar at the time when the group conversions were taking place is necessary to understand

---

[109] G. Pittendrigh and W. Meston, *op. cit.*, 111-112.

the possible motives for conversion. What the missionaries recorded reflect their sympathetic understanding of the contemporary social and economic condition of the Paraiyar in the Chengalpattu area.[110] It was apparent to them that as a group the Paraiyar were ignorant, mostly landless, and lived as serfs, constantly in debt with their daily livelihood entirely controlled and at the mercy of *mirasdars, jamindars* and other caste Hindus. The missionaries had no access to the mind of the Paraiyar. The Paraiyar had no spokespersons or scholars among them to articulate the nature of their spiritual and religious world nor what constituted the core of their culture. Yet without some appreciation of the world of the Paraiyar the emphasis would continue to be on their oppressed status and not on the inner stirrings of an ancient indigenous people, now confronted with a new religion. Were hunger and subjugation sufficient motives to abandon their religion and embrace Christianity? Were they not proud of their religion and rituals? Why did many, even in the same village, not convert to Christianity along with their near and distant relatives? Why did some backslide? Why was the desire for a school a persistent theme in village after village under missionary influence? Answers to these and many such questions will depend upon scholarly studies undertaken with an attitude as if Dalits mattered. Such studies have just begun.[111]

I summarize below some characteristics of the Paraiyar culture that might offer insight into the reasons why some Dalits decided to convert to Christianity. The Paraiyar world is characterized by a certain freedom and equality that men, women and children take

[110] A. Andrew, "The Madras Government and the Pariahs", *The Harvest Field* (1893), 210-216, 241-254; W. Goudie, *op. cit.*

[111] F. J. Balasundaram, *Dalits and Christian Mission in the Tamil Country*; S. Clarke, *Dalits and Christianity: Subaltern Religion and Liberation Theology in India*, Delhi: Oxford University Press, 1999; R. Deliege, *The World of the 'Untouchables': Paraiyars of Tamil Nadu*, Delhi: Oxford University Press, 1997; J. Massey, *Indigenous People: Dalits. Dalit issues in Today's Theological Debate*, Delhi: ISPCK, 1998; Raj Gowthaman, *Dalit Culture* (1993) and *Dalit Perspective of Tamil Culture* (1994), both in Tamil, Gowri Publications, Pondicherry.

for granted. Centralized authority is minimal both within a family and the village. Both sexes share equal skills and spend most of their time outside the house, working in the fields or participating in festivals and entertainment. This gives them a degree of equality found elsewhere only among the tribal society in India. Marriage can be a personal choice, free from dowry with no taboo against divorce or widow marriage, even where the widow already has children. A Dalit woman does not worship her husband as though he is a god. Even in the distant past child marriage was uncommon, and *sati* (widow-burning) was not practised. Religion does not bind them to mandatory and endless rituals, all their lives. Their temple is not in the centre of the hamlet; neither does it occupy a central place in their daily lives. Worship of the mainline Hindu gods was either denied to them or most chose not to worship these gods. The goddesses of the Dalits have the power to possess both the sexes, thus manifesting the divine in the human; they offer wise counsel to people to help them protect their villages and their health, and manage their lives.[112] They can be approached without the mediation of a priestly class. Evil spirits can also take control of an individual. These aspects of the contemporary Dalit culture and religion should have played an important role in the decisions taken by the village collectives and influential leaders to convert to Christianity. Aloysius points out that conversion was a conscious and deliberate move and, "the masses did change over to Christianity only when egalitarianism was clearly on the agenda."[113]

The now surviving elders of descendants have great pride and admiration for their ancestors as intelligent and bold pioneers who decided to take the right step by converting to Christianity. They probably converted not merely to free their people from oppression, low status, poverty and ignorance but also to seek a new identity. They were active agents of a protest movement taking advantage

---

[112] See Iyothee Thass' view of the Buddhist origin of the goddess, Mariamman, in G. Aloysius, *Religion as Emancipatory Identity*, New Delhi: New Age International, 1998, 149.

of what the missionaries were offering. The religion of a white man who touched the untouchable, nursed the afflicted, and gave a decent burial to those who perished in cholera or famine, must surely have love and truth. The anger and pain of endless oppression can now be ignored and their energy and time diverted to this new religion of love. Boys and girls, and men and women, already part of a more egalitarian Paraiyar culture could now sit together and learn and worship. And Sinnakolandai, a Dalit woman, could take the initiative, even if she had to wait for two years, to convert her family members to Christianity. What Christianity offered and Hinduism did not offer, as well as the inherent enabling aspects of the Dalit culture, must have been the animating forces of the group movement of Paraiyar in this region. For hundreds of people conversion to Christianity was a new beginning and a new history.

CHAPTER 3

A DALIT PARISH TO BE REMEMBERED: SAWDAY MEMORIAL CSI CHURCH IN MANDYA, KARNATAKA

Godwin Shiri

Whoever travels to the historic city of Mysore via Bangalore will have to pass through Mandya situated about 105 kms. from Bangalore on the national highway. Once only a taluk headquarters of the larger Mysore District of the old Mysore State, it had until the early decades of this century an appearance of a large village or a market town, mainly for cattle, butter, and cotton weaving. Although the River Kaveri flowed through Mandya area, most of the land was dry and the cultivation was very much dependent on erratic and scanty rainfall.

However, today Mandya is not only the headquarters of Mandya District, it is a fast developing city pulsating with activities. The entire district is now lush with green almost throughout the year with the cultivation mainly of paddy, sugarcane and mulberry. Indeed, Mandya District is known as a granary of Karnataka and has become one of the richest districts of the state. What caused this tremendous change in the topography as well as in the living condition of people? The main cause behind this change was the erection of the famous Krishna Raja Sagar Dam built on the Kaveri River (1924) closer to Mysore City and the subsequent construction of the Vishweshwariah Kaveri River Water Canal (1932) which ensured plenty of water to the Mandya area. Immediately after cultivation activities were accelerated with the construction of the canal, Government started a large sugar factory (1932). After a few years there was yet another large factory, the Mysore Acetate & Chemical Factory, closer to Mandya City. A few more sugar factories were also opened in subsequent years. Thus from the mid-1930s an unprecedented change began taking place in Mandya District.

Mandya is traditionally a stronghold of the Vokkaligas, also known as Gowdas, who are the single largest community in this district. The Vokkaligas are numerous in the southern part of Karnataka and it is well known that they are the key players in Karnataka politics, competing with the Lingayats who are numerous in northern parts of Karnataka. Vokkaligas are Shudras but, as a land-owning community, they are a dominant community. Lingayats and Brahmins, though numerically small, are part of the upper strata in Mandya. The Muslim and Christian religious minorities are also small, but they are in the lower strata like most other backward communities. Scheduled caste people form the second largest community of Mandya district but they are in the lowest strata of society.

The Sawday Memorial CSI Church in Mandya is relatively young, having been established about 75 years ago in 1924. The Church has presently a total of 500 families and it is one of just two pastorates in the entire Mandya District. The other pastorate is located in Kadalore, 28 kilometres north of Mandya city. While about 35 families of the Sawday Church live in about nine out-stations at a distance ranging from five to forty kilometres away, all the rest of the families live in various parts of Mandya city with the bulk, of course, living in the Christian Colony which is situated adjacent to the Church building.

Although the Mandya Church is relatively young, it must be noted that it was only after several decades of missionary labour that it came into existence in 1924. The missionaries as well as the Indian ministers and evangelists of the Wesleyan Methodist Mission frequented the Mandya area from time to time ever since the Wesleyan Mission started its work in Old Mysore State in 1837. After many years of visiting the area, in 1875 the Mission opened a girls' school on Anekere Road and a boys' school in the Dalit Colony in Mandya. In 1878 they opened another school in a neighbouring village called Kyathanagere. The schools brought the people, especially the Holeyas, even closer to the missionaries and to Christian faith. From then onward, regular preaching, Christian instruction, and prayer meetings took place in Mandya, especially in the Dalit colony. Foreseeing the possible conversion of several families, the Mission stationed a native evangelist in Mandya. Two Bible women were also sent from Mysore especially to instruct women and children. Finally, on 30 November 1924, with the baptism of 16 Holeya families (39 adults and 25 children), the Mandya church came into existence. In the following year, namely 1925, 43 baptisms of adults and children took place, further consolidating the new congregation in Mandya. The bulk of the present members of the Mandya Church are the offspring of those first two batches of converts in 1924 and 1925.

CONVERSION AND ITS AFTERMATH

The People

The people who embraced Christian faith in Mandya in 1924 and thereafter were Holeyas, known also as Adi-Karnatakas in recent times. Among the "untouchable" communities of Karnataka, the Holeyas belong to the "right hand" tradition and are more numerous in the southern parts, whereas Madigas belong to "left hand" and are found in larger numbers in northern districts of the state. Whether of the "right" or "left" tradition, they suffer the same inhumane ordeal as victims of the caste system. While both Holeyas and Madigas were (and still are in many of the villages) engaged in a number of menial, traditional occupations like grave-digging, drum-beating, skinning, cobblering, slaughtering, carrying the carrion, scavenging and so on, which were all forced on them, one important difference was that while the Holeyas have long been agricultural labourers, the Madigas were not and their main occupation has always been cobblering. Traditionally Holeyas consider themselves to be superior to the Madigas and normally there exists no social interaction between these two

major Dalit communities. In fact, in state level politics they are
often political rivals.

Historical records indicate that a large number of the Holeyas
of Mandya were engaged in cotton weaving in those days and most
of that business was in the hands of Jains. People would collect
cotton yarn, weave it and return the finished goods, for which they
received a paltry sum. However, the fact that, in addition to
agricultural labour, the Holeyas had acquired some amount of skill
in an occupation (weaving) which was not seen as that degrading,
is something remarkable, a phenomenon generally not found among
Dalits elsewhere. This may be one important reason for the
relatively greater courage and self-confidence found among these
people from the beginning.

Since cotton weaving was not sufficient to sustain their families,
many were also engaged in agriculture as coolies on a full-time or
seasonal basis. A few families owned patches of land; however,
those lands were mostly dry and inferior, and could hardly sustain
them. Therefore the Holeyas of Mandya had to resort to weaving
or agricultural coolie work, or at times both. What is most revealing
is that a large number of people were caught up in a perpetual debt
trap. As a result, not only did they have to mortgage even the little
they owned but they also were forced to become slaves/bonded
labourers (Jeetha) of Vokkaliga landlords, generation after
generation. In general, the condition of Holeyas was extremely
pathetic, as they were forced to live in a socially ostracized/degraded
and economically destitute condition. Their suffering was endless
but it was nobody's business, and in such an inhumane social
environment the missionaries had reached them.

Persecution of the Enquirers and the Converts

After a long period of exposure to the Christian faith, a large number
of Holeya families of Mandya became enquirers, to get ready for
eventual conversion. However, when the news of their plans of
conversion spread, a very strong opposition built up not only in
Mandya but also far beyond it in the Mysore area. Interestingly, it
was a noted Gandhian and Freedom Fighter, Tagadur Ramachandra

Rao, who led this opposition and spread malicious propaganda against missionary work.[1] Pamphlets entitled "The Mischief of Christian Missionaries" were widely distributed and several public meetings were held under his leadership in Mandya, Mysore and elsewhere. Furthermore, they repeatedly promised the leaders of the Holeya community that if they remain as "Hindus," they would be made beneficiaries of special governmental benefits. This did not remain only a promise but was implemented within a few years, dissuading a number of enquirers from taking baptism.

The enquirers and the Native Evangelist were also subjected to more violent victimization by the upper-caste people of Mandya. There were threats, physical assaults and stoning of their place of worship where enquirers used to gather for instruction and prayers. The Native Evangelist, Jeremiah David, was beaten up. Enquirers were harassed mentally and physically in various ways. In spite of all these difficulties, on 30 November 1924, 64 Holeyas came forward and were baptized, laying the foundation of the Christian community in Mandya.

The day the Holeyas were baptized was a day of high drama in Mandya. The town was filled with commotion. There was a threat to set fire to the *pandal* which was erected to conduct the baptisms. Hundreds of curious people from Mandya and the neighbouring villages gathered near the *pandal* to watch the baptism. However, since the missionaries had sought special protection under tight police security, the baptisms were conducted without any untoward incident.

Soon after the baptism a violent tirade was mounted on the converts and the Mission staff.[2] The converts were teased, spoken to in vulgar language, physically assaulted, boycotted from coolie work, taken to police stations on false charges, and their houses and place of worship were stoned. Interestingly, it was not only

[1] N. C. Sargant, *From Missions to Church in Karnataka*, Madras: Christian Literature Society, 1987, 15.

[2] S. Devaputhra, "History of Sawday Memorial Church of Mandya," in S. Sundarappa, ed., *Golden Jubilee Magazine of Sawday Memorial Church*, 1974, 15.

Vokkaligas, Brahmins, Lingayats, Jains and other non-Dalit communities who tormented the converts, but also their own non-convert Holeya kith and kin who actively joined in the tirade. The harassment continued unabated for a year. However, after that direct violence receded to a large extent.

Three points may be made before concluding this section. The first is that it was Rev. G.W. Sawday (1854-1944), the head of the Wesleyan Methodist Mission based in Mysore City, who accepted the Holeya enquirers and personally baptized them. Rev. Sawday, who served as a missionary for 64 years and died in Mysore City, was for a long time a household name among the Christians of the entire Old Mysore State. Said to be of an aristocratic and very wealthy background, Rev. Sawday commanded a great deal of respect from all. The British conferred on him the Kaiser-E-Hind title, an honour for which he was recommended by the Mysore King. His stature certainly helped the enquirers and converts of Mandya and elsewhere to escape from greater atrocity from the casteists and the communalists. Further, Rev. Sawday played a key role in empowering the converts, which will be explained a little later. The Christian community rightly adored him and even now cherishes his memory with gratitude. Not only is the Mandya Church named after him but the Church Community Hall (1974) also bears his name and contains a life-size portrait of him.

However, the Christian community appears to have forgotten the Native Evangelist, Jeremiah David, almost completely. It was David who with outstanding courage and commitment indeed brought the Holeya enquirers into forming a Christian congregation. Stories of his legendary courage still prevail, but only among the diminishing number of very aged members of the Mandya Church. There is nothing that perpetuates the memory of Jeremiah David, who could be rightly named as the co-founder of the Mandya Church along with Rev. Sawday. Interestingly, David was originally of Basel Mission, Mangalore background, a non-Dalit who entered into the service of the Wesleyan Mission during World War I and was stationed in Mandya. It was recorded that he lived in a Vokkaliga locality but worked for the Holeyas, a thing unthinkable in those days when casteist culture ruled supreme.

Second, although most of the nonDalits joined in persecuting the enquirers and converts, it is revealing that it was the goodwill of a few influential caste people which greatly helped the converts in times of deep crisis. One of the persons who came to their support was Kempe Gowda, a well-respected Vokkaliga leader of Mandya. It was recorded that Kempe Gowda carried a personal regard for Jeremiah David, the Native Evangelist. During the height of persecution it was Kempe Gowda who seriously warned and chastised the tormentors. His words prevailed, restraining violence against the converts to a great extent. Furthermore, a Hindu lawyer also supported the converts a great deal by exhorting people about the right to freedom of religion of everyone and urging them not to violate it. However, this Hindu lawyer's name and caste background cannot be traced.

Finally, the conflict between the converted and the non-converted Holeyas inflicted an irrecoverable blow on the unity of these Dalits, who were living as one family. The non-converts blamed their converted kinsmen for desertion and initially they reacted quite violently. True, the caste people of Mandya also instigated the non-converts against the converts, which aggravated the conflict further. On the other hand, the converts charged their non-convert kinsmen as cheeky opportunists who, after getting all benefits including education, health care and even land from the Mission, finally deserted it. The converts seemed to have prided themselves on their new found faith and community; they developed an exclusivistic attitude and subsequently developed a subtly despising attitude towards their unconverted kinsmen. This is unfortunate. Presently there exists no open animosity between the two groups; in fact, there is a good deal of social interaction between the converted and the unconverted Holeyas, but there are no marriage relationships between them. This is quite in contrast to a strong affinity and regular marriage relationship found among converted and unconverted Madigas.[3]

---

[3] Godwin Shiri, *The Plight of Christian Dalits—A South Indian Case Study*, Bangalore: Asian Trading Corporation, 1997, 222.

Empowerment of the Converts

The pastoral care which the Mission provided to the infant church in Mandya was intense. While a Native Evangelist and two Bible women had already been there for some years, an ordained minister was stationed soon after the first baptisms. The pastoral care was fully under the supervision of Rev. Sawday, who was stationed in Mysore. He and other missionaries used to visit Mandya regularly to oversee the pastoral work.

The general content and perspective of pastoral ministry was pietistic. Therefore, there was a special emphasis on the personal holiness of the converts. The pastoral care under Indian ministers and evangelists was literally a surveillance, lest the converts backslide to old social and religious habits. Due to this strict pastoral care, there was steady decline in drinking, small thefts and other such petty crimes and violence among the converts. Further, most of the former religious and social customs and practices, which the missionaries considered superstitious and not in line with the Christian faith, were strictly proscribed. In all these decisions their western, pietistic understanding played the main role. In the initial years many converts were stealthily visiting sorcerers, astrologers and even their former places of worship, but this did not continue for long due to an imposing pastoral ministry of a very protective nature.

However, it must be added that some of the steps the missionaries took in nurturing the converts manifest their wisdom and forethought. Two examples may be mentioned here. One was that most of the Holeyas had names which were either casteist or highly demeaning and insulting, e.g., Chikka, Kulla, Bomma, Bora, Lingi, Sidhi, Kempi. The missionaries replaced these names with well-meaning simple names like Sundara, Sathya, Devadas, Prakasha, Ananda, Sumithramma, Sundaramma, Shanthamma, Shudhamma and so on![4] Interestingly, while in a few cases Biblical names were given to the converts, English names were given only

---

[4] These names mean beauty, truth, light, joy, peace, servant of God, etc.

in very rare cases. The other example was that realizing the need for Indian (Karnatic) music, the missionaries gave foremost importance to it in Christian worship, nurture and missionary preaching. Consequently, even today the Mandya congregation is known for very spirited *Bhajana* singing and many from this congregation have emerged as gifted composers and singers. In fact, the Mandya Christians have developed a talent both in singing and drama (including *Katha Kalaskepha*) over the years, both of which have been important components of the spiritual nurture of these people.

The infant congregation of Mandya was for many years worshipping in a shed-like place of worship. However, in 1937, a full-fledged Church was built close to the new colony, where the converts had been rehabilitated a few years earlier. Almost at the same time a school was built adjacent to the church. With the construction of the church and the school, the formation of the Christian Colony, in which the bulk of the Christian families live, was complete. One remarkable thing about the Wesleyan Methodist Mission was that it gave a top priority to intense pastoral care and always posted well-experienced senior ministers at Mandya. As a result, there was steady progress in all areas of congregational life and soon the Mandya Church became one of the most active churches in the entire Old Mysore State, throbbing with a lot of life and hope.

The congregation of Mandya, coming as it did from utter socio-economic degradation and destitution, was badly in need of all-round empowerment. The contribution of the missionaries to such empowerment was remarkable. True, their theological perceptions were traditional, their spiritual understanding was pietistic, and their socio-economic programmes for the converted were mostly compassion/charity-oriented. A wholistic and liberative perception in their missionary and pastoral work was obviously absent, but many of the programmes they initiated were remarkable and went a long way towards empowering the Church.

When the Mandya Church was established in 1924, most of the members were poor and illiterate cotton weavers, agricultural coolies, serfs and bonded labourers. However, within two decades the congregation had achieved noticeable upward occupational mobility with a sizable number of mechanics, factory hands, carpenters, clerks, teachers and para-medical workers. What caused this change? First and foremost, it was the accessibility to education which caused the change. As noted at the outset, one of the first things the missionaries did was to open three schools in Mandya and in a neighbouring village way back in 1875 and 1878 respectively. Yet one more school was opened adjacent to the new Church in 1937. Thus almost all the children of the first converts got an opportunity to be educated. After the primary level, girls and boys were sent to Mission Boarding schools in Mysore and Tumkur. As a result, there was a tremendous boost in literacy/education, so much so that the once illiterate Christian community has now come to a level almost comparable to the upper castes in this regard. Education obviously provided a large number of people with job opportunities as teachers, clerks, para-medicals, and even factory hands. The fact that the newly converted have also carried a greater motivation and determination to learn cannot be ignored.

A number of other initiatives also helped a great deal in the empowerment of the converted. Rev. Sawday paid the old debts of several bonded labourers and liberated them from the clutches of landlords.[5] He purchased 10 acres of land and rehabilitated the converts in this new place (1935) which has since been named "Christian Colony." Rev. Sawday started a Christian Co-operative Society and helped the families to build their own houses! It is recorded that each family was given a loan of Rs. 350 to build a house. Further, through his personal influence, Rev. Sawday helped in securing loans from banks and co-operative societies in Mandya. He also provided cotton weaving machines to a few families.

The tremendous boost given by the construction of the Vishweshwariah Canal (1932) for the agricultural and industrial activities of Mandya area also helped the Christian community considerably. The newly started sugar factory (1932) absorbed a good number of Christians. Later at one stage, it is said that as

[5] N. C. Sargant, *op. cit.*, 31-32.

many as 30% of the Christian workforce in the parish were employed in this factory. With the construction of KR Sagar Dam and Vishweshwariah Canal, the land-owning Vokkaligas and upper castes became richer, while the up-coming Christian community became a beneficiary. It may be noted that the remarkable boost in agriculture and industry in Mandya district from the 1930s helped the rich to the maximum, while it helped the people in the lower socio-economic strata marginally.

In summing up this section, it may be added that the missionaries' socio-economic initiatives, especially in education, as well as such external factors as the acceleration in agricultural and industrial activities in Mandy, helped the Christian community at a very crucial time of its growth. All these, along with intensive pastoral care, eventually helped the community to acquire a respectable socio-economic status within a span of three to four decades.

THE PRESENT

Today the Mandya Church with 500 families is one of the largest and most active churches in southern Karnataka. At present this church is part of the Karnataka Southern Diocese of The Church of South India which has its headquarters about 300 kms. away in the coastal city of Mangalore. Mandya Christians have migrated to several other places seeking jobs, especially to Mysore City and Bangalore where Mandya Christians are found in large numbers. Wherever they go, they have closely associated with the local churches and actively helped in their growth. Mandya Christians have brought brides from Mysore, Kollegal, Chararajnagar, Tumkur, Hassan and several other places of Old Mysore State. Interestingly, quite a number of brides have been of non-Dalit origin from Mangalore. It is not only that many Christian families have migrated from Mandya, a good number have migrated to Mandya from elsewhere to work in factories and government offices.

The Mandya Church has about nine out-stations, but only an ever-decreasing number of about 35 Christian families live in those places. It is said that out-stations like Besegerahalli and

Kothanahalli had a much larger number of Christian families, but they have gone back to their old religion due to inadequate pastoral care. However, in Mandya city itself hardly any case of reconversion is reported. Of course, there is now a denominational problem. Once it was only the Methodist (now CSI) Church, but there are now over half a dozen other denominations. The Roman Catholic Church was established soon after the Methodist Church in the 1920s. But in recent years Brethren, Pentecostals, Seventh Day Adventists and Jehovah's Witnesses have established their own small congregations. All these sectarian groups together have about 45 families, almost all of them originally from our Mandya Church.

The Mandya Christians are proud of the fact that they are Christians and part of the Church. The religious activities go on throughout the year, with Christmas, New Year time and Good Friday - Easter as the most auspicious occasions for the entire community. Further, revival meetings take place regularly, often more than once a year. The Church has a well-attended Sunday School and quite an active Youth Fellowship, Women's Fellowship and a Bhajana Mandali. The Pastorate Committee, with the Presbyter-in-Charge as Chairman, oversees the entire work of the Church. Since the members take Church activities seriously, many a time group rivalries and conflicts erupt. However, because of the ethnically homogenous nature of the congregation, the conflicts normally do not linger long. Whoever is the pastor of this Church is always a busy person. The enthusiasm of members is such that it will seldom allow the pastor to be idle. The congregation expects their pastor to visit their homes regularly. Christian giving in the congregation is good. People contribute quite generously to special programmes, especially revival meetings.

Several significant general features of this congregation should be noted briefly. One is that the pastoral ministry has always been considered important and continues to be so to a large extent. This is remarkable because in most rural places the pastoral ministry of Dalit congregations has almost totally collapsed.[6] In towns and

---

[6] Godwin Shiri, *op. cit.*, 202 ff.

cities the situation is not much better, as generally there has been a serious lapse.

Another is that the women of the Mandya congregation have over the years become quite well educated and have also developed a great deal of awareness. Quite a large number of them are employed as teachers, para-medical staff, and clerks. Women are regular worshippers, active participants in church activities, and their contribution to the growth of the Church has been significant. However, there is not even a single woman in the 15-member Pastorate Committee! A few years ago, for some time, there were one or two women members in the Committee, but there was none at the time of writing. Another surprising lack is the congregation's contribution to the clergy of the diocese. In spite of the fact that the religious and missionary zeal of Mandya Christians has always been high, seldom have people come forward to take up the ordained ministry. People cite only one or two names in the 75 years of the church's history. This is something unusual and worth probing into.

For the last four decades, Mandya Church has been part of the Church of South India Karnataka Southern Diocese, which has its headquarters in far away coastal city of Mangalore. The diocese has former Basel Mission Christians of non-Dalit origin in the coastal area as well as former Wesleyan Methodist Christians of Mandya and other districts of Old Mysore State who are mostly of Dalit origin. When the Mandya and Mysore area churches were made part of the diocese, there was much opposition because of a fear that the non-Dalit Basel Mission Christians would dominate the diocese. This fear still prevails and most Christians of the Mandya and Mysore area feel that they are always being deprived of resources and leadership opportunities within the Church by the more dominant Mangalore Christians.

A major feature of the history of the Mandya Church is the significant upward socio-economic mobility which the congregation had achieved. This began earlier and has continued at the same pace until recently. The occupational mobility achieved by this community is considerable. Once only poor weavers, agricultural coolies and bonded labourers, today the members are in varied occupations. The occupations of a total number of 358 working men and women are noted in Table 1.

A few important facts in this table need to be highlighted. Nearly a quarter, to be precise 23.4%, of the working force is engaged in education. However, of these 84.5%, are primarily school teachers and 88% are women. Most of the teachers work in government schools. About 10% of the working force is engaged in the para-medical occupations as nurses, midwives, lab technicians, pharmacists, etc. Here again, 80% are women. Of the 10.3% of the working people who are drivers, one is a woman who is an auto driver. There is also a police woman in the congregation.

Table 1

Occupation	Male	Female	Both
Teachers (Primary School)	5	66	71
Teachers (Middle School)	1	7	8
Teachers (High School)	1	1	2
Teachers	1	2	3
Lecturers	1	2	3
Para-medicals (Nurses, ANM, midwives, pharmacists)	7	28	35
Doctors	3	-	3
Business (mostly small, few medium)	29	6	35
Drivers (Government & Private)	36	1	37
Police	2	1	3
Technical work (e.g. mechanic turner, welder, computer operator etc.)	56	1	57
Factory Workers	8	1	9
Class 4 staff (Peons, Attenders, Mali in Government & Private)	34	6	40
Clerical staff (Government & Private)	13	10	23
Government Officers	5	1	6
Coolie Work	14	2	16
Lawyer	1	-	1
Agriculturists	5	2	7
Total	**221**	**137**	**358**

In spite of the noticeable upward occupational mobility achieved, it is revealing that about one-third of the working force is still engaged in occupations which are either low income or unskilled (e.g., Class 4 staff, coolie workers, drivers, and those engaged in technically skilled jobs - Nos. 12, 15, 8 & 10 in the table). However, over the years weaving, which was the original occupation of the majority of the first converts in 1924, and for which once Mandya was well-known, has totally disappeared. Therefore there is no one in the congregation presently engaged in that occupation.

Considering the original deprived condition of the people and the relatively short period of the Church's existence, the occupational mobility achieved by Mandya Christians is quite remarkable. Perhaps in only a few other district headquarter towns/ cities could one find such noticeable upward mobility. However, two brief observations may be made. First, the occupational mobility of the Mandya Christians, which was steadily on an upward move for the past few decades, has stagnated for some years now. The number of teachers working in governmental schools, though quite considerable even now, has steadily decreased. Once a large number of Christians were engaged in the Government Sugar Factory and Acetate Factory, but currently they are a dwindling number there. The same trend could also be seen in the para-medical occupations. It is true that a greater number of Christians are in diversified occupations now, especially in entrepreneurial ones (medium and small business) than was true in the past. While this is a good trend, the fact that there is stagnation in the occupational and economic mobility of the people cannot be ignored. For some years an increasing number of youth have been facing a serious unemployment problem which is creating various problems in family and Church life. It is reported that alcoholism and other such problems are rapidly spreading among the youth.

The other observation is that one of the main reasons why in recent years an increasing number of Christians do not find employment as teachers, para-medical staff and in various other governmental sectors is the Government's reservation policy. More and more qualified people of various castes and communities are taken into employment on a reservation basis. Therefore Christians, who were once taken in larger numbers when competitors were few, are now finding it difficult to get jobs. While this is to be expected, the attitudes of the Christians themselves are also part of the problem. Although the State Government has granted a special quota in education and employment for "Scheduled Caste Converts to Christianity," the Christians in Mandya, as in many other places, do not make use of this provision. Since there is a strong repulsion among them to be identified as people of "untouchable" (Scheduled Caste) origin, seldom do they come forward to avail themselves of the state provisions ear-marked for them. The local church and diocesan leadership do precious little to educate members about those state benefits which are theirs by right. Due to this negative attitude, the Mandya Christians have deprived themselves of many educational and employment opportunities, which is very unfortunate.

SUMMING UP

The Mandya congregation has come a long way from its humble beginnings to its present condition. It is an active congregation and a self-conscious community. They cherish the memory of the pioneers, are grateful to the missionaries, and feel happy to be Christians. Once they were a socially ostracized people, but thanks to the rapid urbanization of Mandya as well as to good economic mobility achieved through the support of the Mission, other communities now treat them "fairly well." Mandya Christians feel happy, even a little proud, to tell the investigator that they now have inter-dining relationships with Vokkaligas and members of other non-Dalit communities. While it is true that there is greater social interaction between Christians and others than existed two or three decades ago, certain hard facts cannot be ignored. To a great majority of non-Dalits, especially those who are members of the upper castes, the Christians are still those "Holeyas," a very insulting and derogatory label laden with casteist prejudice. Although this is rarely expressly stated any more, it is still there deep in their hearts. While in Mandya City Christians do not suffer open caste discrimination any more, it is a fact that the members of the very same Mandya Church living in outstation villages, not too far from the city, are subjected to various forms of open caste discrimination and harassment even today. The general tendency of Mandya Christians is to take such incidents as common occurrences in villages and not to be bothered about them!

Sawday Memorial Church has an active congregation and a self-conscious community in Mandya. The people's enthusiasm is almost limitless, manifested well in the number of Church activities carried on throughout the year. The congregation is also interested in evangelistic work. However, these people, once liberated themselves from the stranglehold of sinful structures and the consequent inexplicable, inhuman conditions, do not seem to be interested in joining hands in the same liberative mission of God. The repulsion they feel about the word "Dalit," their continued alienation from their non-converted Holeya kith and kin, their general attitude of indifference towards the atrocities and the agonies of Dalits, and their excessive interest in gaining social acceptability from upper caste and non-Dalit communities, their unwillingness to avail themselves of state benefits meant for Scheduled Caste Christians (a step which is already proving to be extremely detrimental to the community), all indicate that a much-needed wholistic and liberative understanding of Christian faith and witness is lacking in this Church, including in its pastoral ministry. As a result, the church is showing signs of becoming an inward-looking and self-serving community. This is unfortunate for a congregation which otherwise has had a great history and legacy of courage, determination and motivation.

What are the facts behind the situation? There is more than one factor at work. As noted in the beginning, the Mandya congregation was fruit of the labour of greatly committed and responsible missionaries who came from a pietistic tradition which emphasized personal holiness and other-worldly theological perceptions. In recent decades, the congregation has further succumbed to the influence of still greater emotional piety promoted through the revival preachers who visit regularly. It is sad that the pastors and those who are in leadership positions in the church and in the diocese have done precious little to stop this trend and to impart a more wholistic and contextual faith perception. Therefore, even when a section of the Christian lay men and women have become increasingly socio-politically conscious, the stranglehold of their traditional piety will not allow them to act. Due to all these factors, the Christian community has begun to face a crisis which is spiritual as well as socio-economic in nature and which is likely to deepen further in the years to come. The year 1999 was the 75th anniversary year of the Mandya congregation. It is the right time for the members, lay men and women, pastors and the church leadership, to make a serious examination of the total congregational life which will make them more faithful to their calling.

A Note on Sources

This paper is an outcome of an empirical study of Sawday Memorial CSI Church of Mandya. All the available literature including Church records like Baptismal, Family, Marriage and Burial registers, Proceedings books of the Pastorate Committee, Announcement book, Voters list, Golden Jubilee Magazine (1974) etc., were thoroughly checked. A few Wesleyan Methodist Missionary reports, which are available in the United Theological College Archives in Bangalore, were also consulted. In addition, the pastor, the members of the Pastorate Committee, and a cross-section of 15 members of the Church were personally interviewed through an open-ended questionnaire. The author also participated in the Sunday worship, Youth and Women Fellowship meetings of the church in order to collect relevant data.

CHAPTER 4

PULAYA CHRISTIANS OF KERALA: A COMMUNITY IN A DILEMMA

George Oommen

The purpose of this study is to portray significant aspects of change and continuity in the life of a small Pulaya Christian congregation. The Kottankudi congregation of the Church of South India is exclusively a Pulaya congregation of about 55 families. It is situated seven kilometres from Mallappally, a Syrian Christian stronghold in Central Kerala, on the Mallappally-Ranni Road. The main focus of the study will be on the period from 1920 to 1998, for which sources are available.

A word about the sources is not out of place. I decided to choose this particular congregation without any prior knowledge about available sources and I was determined to work with anything which was in written or empirical form. I ended up handling some rich written sources in the form of a Baptismal Register (1930-1998), Rent Collection Records (1951 onwards), Membership Register (1951 onwards), Service Register (1921-1940 and 1968-1995), and Marriage Register (1970-1998). I have chosen to concentrate mainly on the "occupation" column of the different registers as well as on the land records with a view to finding indicators of upward mobility. Further, both the Service Register and the Membership Register provide information on the state of pastoral and ministerial care. The most valuable section in the Membership Register was the 'Remark' section on each of the 55 families in the parish. If read together with other information, the comments by different evangelists and pastors are indeed revealing. In addition, I have interviewed several members of the parish, one of whom is the great grand old man who has been the sexton for the last several decades.

Pulayas or Cherumar, the agricultural labour "outcastes" and one of the lowest status groups in old Kerala, rate themselves a cut above the Parayas. Pulayas are numerically the larger of these scheduled castes in the Kerala list. Missionary work aimed at bringing Pulayas into the Anglican Communion reached its peak in the latter half of the 19th century. Dalits constituted more than half of the membership of the Diocese of Travancore and Cochin in 1947 when it became the Madhya Kerala Diocese of the Church of South India. In the midland regions of Travancore (a princely state) and the highlands to the east, they worked as farm hands raising paddy, tapioca and cash crops. In the paddy fields of the west coast, they were ploughers of the soil, sowers of seeds, transplanters of seedlings, removers of weeds, irrigators, harvesters, dryers of grain and loaders into the safe wooden storage vaults of the Syrian Christian and Nair landowners' houses. Both men and women participated in all operations from the field to the barn and cellar.

Most Pulayas were agricultural labourers and were held in bondage (*adima*) or in a client relationship with their high caste landlords. Part of the "privilege" of being in such a client relationship was the right to claim bare maintenance from the landlords, and a small share in the produce of the land. It was a highly exploitative and oppressive system. In his journal on December 5, 1850, George Matthan, a Syrian Christian priest, presented the "unparalleled" conditions of the Pulaya "slaves" by highlighting their inhuman treatment by Nair and Syrian Christian landlords, as well as their poverty and misery as follows:

> The condition of these unhappy beings is, I think, without a parallel in the whole range of history. They are regarded as so unclean, that they are thought to convey pollution to their fellow creatures, not only by contact, but even by approach. They are so wretchedly provided with the necessities of life that the most loathsome things are a treat to them. Their persons are entirely at the disposal of their masters, by whom they are bought and sold like cattle, and are often worse treated. The owners had formerly power to flog and enchain them, and in some cases to maim them, or even deprive them of their lives ...

They were everywhere paid for their labour at the lowest possible rate.[1]

The CMS missionaries, who came to Travancore in 1816, were by the 1850s acquainted with social conditions in Travancore, and especially with the sufferings of the Dalits. The early 1850s was a period when CMS missionaries campaigned vigorously against the *adima* (bonded labour) system. Missionary propaganda about its disabilities and miseries brought the attached labourer system into disrepute. This finally ended in the emancipation of the slaves. On 24 June 1855 it was declared that owning slaves was illegal.[2]

Following the emancipation of the slaves in Travancore in 1855, Pulayas and Parayas from different parts of Travancore approached the CMS missionaries or their representatives with requests for "Christian instruction" and "slave schools," clearly indicating their readiness to move to a new religion and further their alliance with the missionaries. Thus commenced the Dalit Christian conversion movement in central Travancore in 1855. Mallappally was one of the major centres of these mass conversion movements and the parish under study is a typical centre of the Pulaya movement in the latter half of the 19th century.[3]

BEGINNING OF THE CONGREGATION

None of the surviving records or the "super human" memories of the elderly among the present members could provide any accurate details regarding the beginnings of the parish. By contrast, people in the surrounding Syrian Christian parishes "know everything"

[1] The Missionary Register, 1852, 444f.

[2] See J. W. Gladstone, *Protestant Christianity and People's Movements in Kerala 1850-1936*, Trivandrum: Seminary Publications, 1984 and Dick Kooiman, *Conversion and Social Equality in India, The London Missionary Society in South Travancore in the 19th Century*, New Delhi: Manohar Publications, 1989.

[3] See for details George Oommen, "Dalit Conversion and Social Protest in Travancore 1854-1890," *Bangalore Theological Forum*, XXVIII (September-December 1996), 69-84.

about their beginnings. Family histories, which trace their Christian beginnings back to the St. Thomas tradition, and jubilee history souvenirs are countless. Then how and why does a Dalit parish not have a definitive idea about their beginnings? Are they not concerned about such things or is this a manifestation of the utter neglect which Dalit congregations suffer at the hands of the dominant Syrian Christians? I have no specific answer to offer to these questions. However, the information, which many Pulaya informants very clearly hold in their memories and oral narratives, is indeed revealing and historically significant.

Firstly, the congregation members' oral history traces the beginnings of this parish back to the time of the emancipation of the slaves. They would say, "Our forefathers were converted to Christianity when sahibs (*saippanmar*) liberated them from slavery." This is a common narrative. They do not know when it happened. If you probe for details about the English missionaries in the locality, they may keep silent. However, the emotional tone with which they narrate it is sufficient to convince any skeptical modern historian that it is the story of their Christian beginnings.

Circumstantial evidence and my own personal knowledge of the locality help me trace the beginnings of the congregation to some time between 1860 and 1880. Many other Dalit congregations emerged in this area during the same period. Missionary reports refer to this as Mallappally, a Syrian Christian area where the first Pulaya conversion took place in 1854. C. M. S. missionary reports also link the founding of several Pulaya congregations to the mass conversions that followed the anti-slavery movement of the 1850s.

The actual and direct involvement of a European missionary in the origins and the ongoing life of this congregation might be half myth and half fact. The Service Register reveals that only three missionaries had visited the parish since 1921. However, those visits were the greatest occasions in the life of the congregation. In 1921 when W.S. Hunt visited, 140 people attended the service and in 1928 Bishop E. A. L. Moore's visit attracted 350 people to the church. Yet the average attendance at a service was only sixty during that period. Why was there such a mass response during these special visits? This may give us some clue to the continuing attachment and emotional alliance that existed between missionaries and Dalits during the last decades of the nineteenth century.

The missionary link also had a subversive dimension. Any open declaration of association with the Anglican Church and its missionaries was considered to be a "subversive action" on the part of the Pulayas. Along with Christianity, the C. M. S. missionaries were acquiring a special place in the life of the Pulaya community. In the context of the emotion-laden conflicts of the period, Hawksworth, a nearby missionary, observed, "some of them speak as if they had at length found a friend—a friend that sticketh closer than a brother," in the CMS missionary.[4] We can see the traces of this emotion still lingering in the minds and in the current narrative which the present members of the parish give of their Christian origins.

A second piece of information, which the local congregation provides, is that they have had a school-cum-worship place as far as their memory goes. Education and literacy, which were unprecedented in their experience, are very much a part of their memory. Most Pulaya communities who sought out a missionary first asked for the establishment of a "school" and a "teacher." The congregation under study did have and continues to have a lower primary school. This was a major source of their initial momentum. However, as we shall see later, this literacy programme did not provide them with any concrete socio-economic upward mobility until recent times.

Thirdly, the landed property in which the community was settled constitutes an important component in the oral narratives of Christian beginnings. By the 1920s almost all the families in the congregation were occupying the 40 acres of land attached to the Kottankudy congregation. What is the significance of land in the life of these Dalits?

It was a widespread practice of the C. M. S. missionaries to acquire land from the government in the remote, uninhabitable hills

---

[4] Hawksworth, in *The Missionary Register*, 1852, p. 444.

to settle newly converted Dalits. A. F. Painter acknowledged that "parcels of unused land for settlement" were offered to missionaries by the Travancore Government due to missionary influence.[5] Scattered references in missionary correspondence suggest that by the 1880s the C. M. S. had acquired land at various places in Central and Northern Travancore to settle Dalit converts. By 1931 the C. M. S. owned 4000 acres of land.[6] In the Mallappally area, one of the Pulaya converts' major centres, the C. M. S. had 124 acres of land.

It should be noted that there was no radical "resettlement" of Dalit converts according to which they were moved far away from their traditional village homes. They were resettled within the same locality in which they already lived, so that they could continue as labourers for the same landlords as before. However, the parcels of land on which they were settled were safely distanced from those of the landlords so as to keep the "untouchable" Pulaya converts in isolation. In all these C. M. S. lands the newly settled families had to pay the *pattom* (rent) to the Church, which in effect emerged as their new landlord. These Pulaya Christian families thus had hereditary tenancy rights to these C. M. S. lands, even though they continued to labour on other lands for other landlords as well.

The acquisition of land had wide implications for a Pulaya "ex-slave." Few Pulayas had private landed property due to the dispossession they experienced as untouchables. Furthermore, by custom Pulayas lived and worked on the property of their landlords or "masters," practically excluding them from the right to possess their own land. At Kottankudy 33 families were paying rent to the local church in 1951 and had been occupying plots of varying sizes from 40 cents to 4 1/2 acres. This constituted two-thirds of the 55 families who were affiliated to this congregation.[7]

[5] Painter, 28 December 1889, Church Missionary Society, *Annual Letters 1889-1890*, 127.

[6] P. T. David, *Mahayidavaka Jubilee Smarakam*, Kotayam, 1930, 201.

[7] Rent Collection Records 1952; The Membership Register, 1951.

It is significant to note that although almost all of the congregation households were landholders, in the 1930s only a tiny minority acknowledged that they are cultivating their own land. Until the early 1950s a substantial majority of the parents whose children were being baptized entered their occupation as "coolie" in the Baptismal Register. Circumstantial evidence and information gained from interviews indicate that a substantial majority was not carrying out any agricultural operations on their own landed property. Why were they not cultivating their land, a proud possession? This reveals something about the Pulayas' traditional attitude toward land ownership and cultivation. They had been landless agricultural labourers for generations who were now entering into the sphere of the cash economy. They do not seem to have become cultivators of their own land. In fact, it is clear from the available data that they started farming their own land for additional income generation only after the 1950s. However, we may note that this was happening while many continued as agricultural labourers. By the middle of the 1960s a majority of the parents used the word *krishi* (cultivation) to refer to their occupation, indicating an increase in the number of householders who were depending on their own land for additional income.

However, the most significant change evident in the land records pertains to the alienation of these landed properties. My investigation revealed that roughly less than half of the original 42 acres remains in the hands of Pulaya Christians. A substantial majority of the new legal owners of the alienated land are Syrian Christians. While seven Syrian Christian families now occupy this alienated property, only one Dalit family had managed to buy a portion of it. This might have happened as a result of mortgage and loans from C. S. I. Pulaya Christians.

While the alienation of lands previously occupied by members of the congregation can be perceived as a sign of degradation, there is another side to the story. For several decades this locality was known as a *Pulayakudi* and there were hardly any others living there. With increased population pressure and increases in land value, poor Syrian Christians and members of other high castes were ready to buy land in areas previously designated as Dalit colonies. Thus the demographic character of this locality has been undergoing a tremendous transformation. This has several other implications. In this process of change the "ex-untouchable" Christian is becoming more and more "touchable" and social interaction between Pulaya Christians and members of the high castes is increasing.

Before we move on to the next issue, it may be relevant to note that the average size of the C. S. I. Pulaya Christian land holdings is less than an acre. This happened as a consequence of redistribution of inherited land among the sons of the original families. However, in a state like Kerala, where land is an asset, these Dalit Christians are in a more advantageous situation than are many of the landless agricultural labourers among them.

UPWARD OCCUPATIONAL MOBILITY

As noted earlier, until 1945-1946 almost all the parents of the children baptized indicated that their "occupation" was "coolie" or "coolie worker" (coolie or coolie *vela*) despite the fact that a majority of them were small landholders. By 1950 a substantial number, although not a majority, referred to their occupation as "cultivation" (*krishi*). From 1959 onward "coolie" and "coolie worker" categories began to disappear from use in the documents to be replaced by *karshakathozhilali*, which literally means agricultural labourer. This was a very clear goodbye to a title of degradation and a deliberate choice of a more dignified occupational category.[8] The Communist Party's elevation to power in 1957 in Kerala and influence among Dalit Christians is evident in the name change, as these symbolized a changing self-perception and aggressiveness brought about by the empowerment of Dalits.[9] As

[8] Baptismal Register.

[9] See George Oommen, "Communist Influence on Dalit Christians— The Kerala Experience," in Kanichikattil Francis, ed., *Church in Context: Essays in Honour of Mathias Mundadan CMI*, Bangalore: Dharmaram Publications, 1996, 31-55; see also T. K. Oommen, *From Mobilisation*

a result, most of the Pulaya Christians in these regions became the co-travellers of the Communist Party.

If we take the "occupational" column in different Church Registers as an indicator of occupational mobility among congregation members, we can see dramatic developments taking shape within the Kottankudy Dalit community. By the 1960s a gradual shift was occurring, almost "silently." For the first time two job categories began to appear occasionally, those of evangelists and teachers. Entries in the teacher category do not reveal the institutions to which the teachers are affiliated; we can only assume that they were C. S. I. School teachers. Thus even in the 1960s the Church seemed to be the major provider of occupational change for some of its members. In addition, two people were in military service jobs.[10]

From 1950 to 1970, eight people in the congregation were either teachers or evangelists, while eight others were printers, government clerks, tailors, or in military service. Between 1970 and 1998, eleven people were being referred to as teachers or evangelists and 22 others indicated that their occupations were clerks, government service, mason, postman, company worker, autorickshaw driver, etc.[11] It is evident that there is a steady increase in the number of people who were leaving their traditional occupation and relying on non-agricultural work for their income. This is an indication of the community's upward mobility.

My personal inquiry shows a dramatic increase in the number of educationally qualified people in recent times. There are eight graduates, one diploma holder in engineering and one post-graduate in the congregation at present. Except for two, however, none of them were able to translate this education into income-generating

to Institutionalisation: The Dynamics of Agrarian Movement in Twentieth Century Kerala, Bombay: Popular Prakashan, 1985, for communist influence on agrarian movements in Kerala.

[10] Baptismal Register, Marriage Register, Interviews.

[11] Marriage Register, Interviews with groups and individuals, January 1999.

jobs.[12] The reasons for this stagnation are the high unemployment
rate in the state and the Dalit Christians' non-eligibility for jobs
reserved for the Scheduled Castes. Many of them feel frustrated
about this situation. Considering that one of the major aspirations
of a Dalit Christian has been to educate his or her children to the
highest level possible, the situation is indeed frustrating. Their
typical feeling is that the Church and State have betrayed them by
denying them job opportunities, while high caste people dominate
the available job market.[13] However, the most interesting aspect
of the present situation of stagnation is that education is still
considered by many to be the main prerequisite for a rise in status.
So, despite the fact that education does not automatically become
an income earning resource, parents still insist on their children
reaching higher educational levels.

PASTORAL CARE

There is a general perception among the dominant C. S. I. Syrian
Christians that Dalit Christians are less active within the Church
and are less committed to Christianity. They feel that conversion
movements have only created half-baked Christians out of Dalits.
This perception bears examination, especially with reference to
this local congregation.

Almost all of the Christian care and nurture of this congregation
was entrusted to an evangelist until 1990 when it was elevated to
a pastorate. A well-educated Dalit presbyter was appointed as its
first vicar. It is enough to note that little pastoral care was actually
available to these people until his appointment; they were treated
as second class citizens within the pastoral care structure of the
diocese.[14] During the years 1921-1941, a nearby Syrian Christian
pastor celebrated an average of four Holy Communions per year
and each time he would return to his own parish immediately after
the service. Between 1968 and 1989 the average number of Holy

---

[12] Interview with the Pastor, January 1999.
[13] Interview, January 1999.
[14] Service Register.

Communions and pastoral visits per year increased to seven, indicating an improvement. The increase in average Holy Communions and pastoral visits do not seem to have translated into an increase in the members' participation in the Holy Communion. In fact, the average number of people receiving Holy Communion in these services declined from 27 during 1921-1941 to 25 during 1968-1989. As I did not have access to the total number of eligible communicants in the congregation, it is difficult to ascertain why this was so.[15] However, there was a general improvement in the regular attendance of members in the regular Sunday worship after the congregation was raised to the level of a pastorate. This is also reflected in the participation in Holy Communion. During the 1990s the average numbers indicate an almost 100% increase.[16]

The movement of families to other denominations such as the Pentecostals, Salvation Army, and Roman Catholicism is to be seen as integrally related to the nature of pastoral care. The information gathered from the "Remarks" section of the Membership Register reveals that about twelve families left the church to join other denominations, a substantial majority becoming Pentecostals. In addition, seven families are virtually inactive within the life of the congregation even though they remain members. A handful of families also left for faraway places.[17].

The most recent remarks of the Presbyter regarding the involvement of members in the total life of the congregation indicate the highly unsettled nature of their Christian identity and involvement. In 1992-1993, the bishop excommunicated an entire joint family because one son joined the Salvation Army, while another daughter and son are practicing Hindus who got married in a temple according to Hindu rites. The same pastor referred to members who have never participated in the Holy Communion as well as to several others who have not been confirmed. The total

[15] Service Register.
[16] Service Register.
[17] Membership Register.

picture that emerges is very mixed. I have noted that out of the 55 families listed, 20 have some problem or the other with the local church.[18] What is the reason for this situation? It can be assumed that while the majority are gradually being assimilated into highly structured and liturgical worship patterns, mostly influenced by Anglo-Syrian traditions, a good number, through their inactivity, defection, migration and movement across religious and denominational boundaries are expressing an attitude of dissatisfaction. They seem to be saying that the pastoral and worship patterns do not cater to their emotional and cultural needs.

What do Pentecostal or independent churches provide Pulaya Christians that they do not receive in C. S. I. congregations? Two things may be stated. The first is that the Pentecostals provide for the sustenance of communitarian values. Pulayas, culturally and religiously, belong to a corporate community where meaningful community living and sharing shape much of their life. Emotional and social needs are taken care of within such structures, whereas the C. S. I. gives prominence to a few individuals and creates a hierarchy within the community. The second is that mainstream churches such as the C. S. I. do not seem to provide meaningful avenues for Dalits to express and utilize their pre-Christian religiosity and culture. My interviews with the people reveal that many Pulaya Christians are very sensitive about the issue of sorcery and beliefs related to spirits. The traditional, primal belief systems and worldview still persist in their minds. Two families in the congregation have explained to me how *shukdram* (black magic) can have a negative impact on people, although they themselves do not perform these rituals. The evil impact of spirits is still real to many Pulaya Christians. A former church warden, the present vicar, and some other members (including some women) acknowledged that many are moving to Pentecostalism because it provides space for the traditional communal lifestyle and ample means to revive their pre-Christian religious belief systems. The esoteric practices of some Pentecostal pastors are also a great attraction to many. Moreover, the activities and language of the

[18] Membership Register.

Pentecostals recapture many of the traditional views of Dalit Christians.

RELATIONSHIP WITH SYRIAN CHRISTIAN NEIGHBOURS

Considering the fact that Pulaya Christians suffered almost all the consequences of untouchability, the picture that emerges now is profoundly different than before. Recollecting how, within his own experience, members of the high castes treated Pulaya Christians, the 84 year-old present sexton told how he and his wife had to shout, "hoi, hoi" to warn the high castes of their presence. This was done so that the high castes could remain at a distance in order to avoid pollution. He also said that it took a good portion of a day to walk the seven kilometres to reach Mallappally, the main town, and now he can travel there freely by bus.[19]

The change is dramatic and the present relationships between Syrian Christians and Pulaya Christians stand in stark contrast to the practices of the past. Local Syrian Christians now-a-days attend Pulaya Christian weddings and even participate in the wedding feasts arranged in Pulaya Christian houses. This was unimaginable about 15 to 20 years ago. How do we explain this change? One of the former church wardens, K. M. Joseph, whose daughter's wedding several Syrian Christians attended, said, "If my house is fairly well kept in clean surroundings and the food is prepared in a clean and Syrian Christian style, they would attend. Otherwise these fellows will give one excuse or the other and leave immediately after the wedding ceremony at the Church."[20]

However, the dilemma of the Pulaya Christian community is very clearly depicted in one of K. M. Joseph's recent experiences. After his painting job in one of the Syrian Christian houses, he was invited to sit along with the male members of that family for a meal, an unprecedented action. However, he noticed that his fellow

[19] Interview, K. M. Joseph, 68 years.
[20] Interview, K. M. Joseph, 68 years.

church member, who is a "coolie worker," was served food outside on the verandah and was seated on the floor. Joseph was in a serious dilemma and did not accept food again during his painting contract. His explanation for the dilemma is indicative of the predicament of the whole community. To him, the incident showed that Syrian Christians are ready to accept Pulaya Christians in certain areas if they imitate the Syrian Christians' lifestyle. However, he went on to say, "If Syrian Christians do not accept our community as a whole, why should I find happiness in this better treatment to me as an individual?"

This incident demonstrates that, on the one hand, Pulaya Christians are very much caught up in the language of caste and community and, on the other hand, they are under tremendous pressure to emulate Syrian Christian ways in order to be accepted across caste boundaries. Joseph, one of the most articulate persons in the congregation, sums up the present situation of Dalit Christians as follows: "We are neither there nor here." These words depict not only the dilemma within which the local Pulaya Christian community is caught up, but also the tremendous existential pressure under which they are experiencing upward mobility.

CONCLUSION

The local Dalit Christian community is caught up in three types of dilemmas. 1) They are under pressure from Syrian Christians to follow the Syrian Christian pattern of life in the socio-religious sphere. Dalit Christians have to eat, speak and dress like Syrian Christians in order to be accepted. At the same time their emerging collective identity and Dalitization is pulling them in the opposite direction. The Dalit solidarity and self- assertion movements of the 1990s are having a profound impact on their caste militancy.[21] Dalitness is seen by many as a source of empowerment and strength rather than as something to be ashamed of. There seems to be a

---

[21] See Paul Chirakarod and others, *Dalit Kavithagal: Oru Padanam*, Tiruvalla: C. S. S., 1992; Paul Chirakarod, *Dalit Kraisthavar Keralathil*, Tiruvalla: C. S. S., 2000.

tension between Syrianization, (imitation of Syrian Christian life-style and value systems), and Dalitization processes recently.

2) The upward mobility of Dalit Christians is evident in an unprecedented manner. Higher educational qualification are definitely helping many to give up their caste occupation, which traditionally offered them only a "coolie worker" status, but they are unable to get into the job market due to the denial of Scheduled Caste status. Despite the high rate of unemployment and a state of stagnation in upward mobility, education is high in the community's agenda. Their self-perception is that education provides the best means for them to gain social acceptance, dignity, and a sense of self-worth.

3) A subtle but a real dilemma exists regarding their pre-Christian belief and cultural systems. The present structures of pastoral care do not provide enough space for these to survive. Movements between boundaries, both religious and denominational, are only expressions of this dilemma. While a substantial number of Dalit Christians are accepting Syrianization as a means to get out of this dilemma, many others are refusing to do so.

CHAPTER 5

DALIT CHRISTIANS IN BHALEJ, GUJARAT

Raj Kumar Hans and Siddhi Macwan

Bhalej is a fairly big village in Umreth *taluka* of Anand district in central Gujarat. It lies 13 kilometres from Anand on a broad-gauge railway line between Anand and Godhra, which is a major junction on the Bombay-Delhi line of Western Railways. According to the 1991 census, the village has 1562 hectares of land and a population of 12,070 (2030 households). Muslims make up 65% of the total population. Of these the Maliks, Thakores, Vohras (all farmers) and Khatkis/Quresh (butchers) occupy around 200 houses each, while the Pathans have about 55 houses, the Sayyids about 35, the Kazis about 35, Faqirs about 30, and Khalifa (barbers) about 20 houses. The Muslims, being the majority in the village, have been able to win the position of *sarpanch* for their community for the first time. Ms. Zubedabibi Yakubali Sayyid is the present *sarpanch*. However, apparently the Muslims are not the real wielders of power. The Patidar Patels, represented by their leader Jasbhai Mangalbhai Patel, are in "real" control of the village affairs. The fact that the Muslim majority has been excluded from political power is due to their overall relative poverty in comparison to the affluence of the Hindu minority. This contrast is primarily due to local economic relations but is also affected by power equations prevailing in the state. Among Hindus the Leuva Patels (farmers) have 250 houses, Ravalji Darbars (Rajputs) have 80, Brahmans 25, Vania 35, Harijans 40, Chamars (leather-workers) about 8, Barots (genealogists) about 15, Valand (barbers) about 10 houses. There are a few other smaller caste/professional groups. There are also 15 Jain households in the village.

Christians are numerically the third largest segment of the village, accounting for about 150 houses. There are four denominations of the Christian Church active in Bhalej. Roman Catholics have 65 families and the Salvation Army has 50 families. The Methodists have two families in the village and about 50 houses in a separate locality of Bhalej called Badapura. There are 17 Church of North India (C. N. I.) families who also reside in an independent colony called Sheledipura or Vishwasipura. All four denominations have church buildings for their congregations, the oldest being the C. N. I. Church built in 1878, then known as IP (Irish Presbyterian) Mission Church. The next church building to be built was the Methodist Church, constructed in 1887. The Salvation Army Church was built in 1899 and renovated in 1968, while the Roman Catholic Church was the last to be built in 1938. A resident pastor, Arvind Christian, serves the Salvation Army congregation. Rev. Santray Philip serves the C. N. I. Church and Pastor Pravinbhai looks after the religious needs of the Methodists. The Catholics do not have a resident priest but Father Mickey Guedes comes to Bhalej from Anand twice a month for the mass. The Roman Catholics have a primary school which goes up to the fifth standard. There is a Primary School, an Urdu school up to seventh standard, an Anjuman High School, and 4 *madrasas*, all run by the Muslims. Besides these, there are government schools including a higher secondary school.

Bhalej was selected for this study because it happened to be one of the first localities where mass conversions had taken place during the last decade of the nineteenth century. The Irish Presbyterian Mission had started evangelistic work in the village in the 1870s, converting some local Dalits, inducing others to settle and cultivate 300 acres of land which the missionary had procured in the village. Very soon a church was consecrated giving the new community a distinct identity. It was still a small community in 1890 when a movement began that changed the situation drastically as far as the Irish Presbyterian missionaries were concerned. Along with other members of the Bhangi community, the lowest in the Hindu caste hierarchy, one Karsan Ranchhod of Bhalej had gone to Bombay in the early 1880s in search of jobs. They easily got jobs as sweepers. In Bombay they came in touch with some Methodist missionaries and 19 of them were converted. Two years later they visited their homes where their newly gained confidence excited the curiosity of the villagers. This first batch of Methodist Christians inspired the missionaries to give special attention to Bhalej. This led the Mission to build a church in 1887 and to organize some grand religious festivals for the purpose of conversion. The first in a series of *melas* they organized was held at Bhalej in 1895 when about 300 people who had been previously instructed were baptized. The mass conversion was facilitated further by the severe famines of 1899-1901. In 1903 another *mela* was organized in Bhalej at which Bishop Thoburn baptized "thousands" by sprinkling water on people belonging to the Dhed, Vankar and Bhangi castes, all at one time (These "thousands" did not necessarily belong to Bhalej village). Yet another festival was organized in 1906. The tide of mass conversion seems to have ebbed thereafter. The Roman Catholics, who appeared on the Bhalej scene in the second decade of the century, failed to attract any new converts. Instead, by extending some material help they were able to lure some people who were already Christians into their fold. This is clearly borne out by the elders of the community. In Bhalej the major losers happened to be the commanders of the Salvation Army.

The fact that there have been four denominations active in the village for over a century led us to think that Bhalej would offer us an excellent opportunity to situate the present condition of the Dalit Christians in Gujarat. The Bhalej Christians came predominantly from Dalit (Dheds, Vankars, Chamars, Bhangis etc.) backgrounds and include only a sprinkling from the middle castes like Garasia and Patanwadia Rajputs. The present study, which attempts to understand and map out various levels of change affecting the Dalit converts in Bhalej as well as in Gujarat generally, is based upon meetings and interviews with the village leaders, pastors, and community members belonging to different faiths, but has also been informed by general readings on the theme.

The conversion movement, which was so vibrant in the first half of the twentieth century, came to a stop in the 1950s because of some major changes which occurred in the years following

Independence. Anti-untouchability laws, reservations for the Scheduled Castes, increased urbanization, speedy industrialization, the expansion of schools and hospitals, improved means of communications, spatial and occupational mobility, initiated a process that blunted the edge of social degradation. The state took up many of the activities traditionally done by missionary organizations, like running schools, hospitals, relief and development programmes on such a broad scale that the work and contribution of the missionaries was dwarfed by comparison. Although there are cases of a few converts going back to the Hindu fold elsewhere in Gujarat, not a single case has been reported in Bhalej. The kind of self-respect and confidence gained by the Christians here, consolidated by the active priesthood over a period of time, did not warrant any such move.

The Christians of Bhalej owing allegiance to four different denominations are primarily engaged in agriculture. The vast majority work as landless labourers but there are also some independent farmers with small landholdings. The latter belong mainly to the C. N. I. Church and inhabit the autonomous and nucleus settlement in the fields called Sheledipura. Those 17 Christian houses enjoy an air of independence and dignity hard to find among the majority of Christians who are surrounded by and dependent upon rich people of other faiths. Similar is the case of a Methodist family of the Karsandas lineage. There are also a few Christians in the services and over the years around 40-45 families have moved to the cities. Though our observations are focused upon the village Christians, we have taken a comparative view, keeping both the changes affecting the village Hindu Dalits and changes witnessed among urban Gujarati Christians in mind. Without these comparisons we could give a lopsided picture of the whole process of change among rural Dalit Christians.

The story of Karsandas Ranchhod's family offers interesting insights into the process of transformation through religious change. Our informant, Mr. Sylvester Isaac, belongs to the fourth generation of descendents of the legendary Karsandas Ranchhod. Karsandas, as earlier referred to, was a Bhangi. The Methodist mission had apparently procured land for a detached colony of new Christians. This small colony, known as Karsanpura, is situated about two kilometres from Bhalej proper, as is the other detached Christian colony, Sheledipura. The ruins of the outer walls of the Karsanpura settlement show how originally it could have been a safe and thriving enclave of converts. The church building, now over a hundred years old, is a beautiful but abandoned site along with an equally spacious two-storey quarter for the pastor. A well was constructed for drinking and irrigation purposes a hundred years ago. The inscription in Gujarati on a stone slab fixed on the well states that Karsan Ranchod erected it in Samvat 1952 (CE 1895) on his own without anybody's partnership at a cost of Rs. 1250.

Karsandas Ranchhod had two sons, Bhula Karsan and Chhagan Karsan. While Bhula's son, Isaac, continued tilling the land given to Karsan, Chhagan's son, Emmanuel, is said to have moved to Ahmedabad. Emmanuel's elder son, Wilfred, is currently the pastor at Dabhoi, a town 20 kilometres east of Baroda. Sylvester owns 20 *bighas* of prime land. He has two sons and a daughter. His daughter, Stella, is studying in an Irish Presbyterian Mission boarding school at Anand, 14 kilometres away. Sylvester owns a motorbike as well as a new Tata Sumo jeep. He is an earnest Christian but is pained by the indifference which the Methodist Church establishment has shown towards the congregation and is highly critical of the clergy for neglecting the spiritual needs of the congregation. It is true that a majority of the Methodists have moved out of Karsanpura to pursue better prospects in the nearby towns and cities, and have left behind only farming families. That is perhaps why the pastor has been withdrawn from the locality. What pains Sylvester Isaac even more, however, is the way the District Superintendent wanted to dispose of the Church property.

The Methodists of Karsanpura are illustrative of an important process of change. For them conversion led to land ownership, moderate wealth, and social mobility through emigration to the towns and cities. Emigration in turn has led to the demise of the church, as there were too few Methodists left to warrant a full-time pastor and an active congregational life. However, the

Methodists of Karsanpura are not typical of the Dalit Christians of Bhalej as a whole. While the ancestors of the others may have used conversion as a form of protest and struggle against, as well as an alternative to their social degradation within the oppressive socio-economic and religious order, their present economic condition in the village does not indicate that conversion sufficiently helped to elevate their economic status. They have remained stagnant in economic life, with the exception of those very few who moved out to the cities. A significant section of the Hindu Dalits who became Christians continued to live alongside Hindu Dalits within the same village. After over a century's experience, there exist now varying degrees of religious, cultural and economic distance between them which can be attributed to the religious factor. The converts benefited in the pre-Independence period from the modernization package delivered through the educational and economic institutions associated with the missionaries. However, in the post-Independence period, because of the affirmative action benefits constitutionally guaranteed to them, the pace of advancement among Hindu Dalits has been comparatively faster than among Christian Dalits. It has been observed that in some of the villages in Gujarat, there are Dalit Christians who have conveniently adopted a dual identity in order to secure those benefits of the Government's reservation policy denied them because of their religion. However, there is not a single case of a Bhalej Christian who has taken advantage of Scheduled Caste benefits. On the contrary, the Christians here take great pride in their religious identity, as over the decades it has earned them greater respect from the high caste Hindus.

In 1972 the Government of Gujarat appointed the Socially and Educationally Backward Class (SEBC) Commission to identify Other Backward Classes (other than the Scheduled Castes and Scheduled Tribes) in Gujarat. Its report, published in 1976, identified about eighty caste groups for ameliorative measures. One of them happens to be "Gujarati Christi" (Gujarati Christians). Though this was received with enthusiasm by rural Christians, it was resented by urban Christians, especially those in the middle income group. To be labelled "backward"' would mean losing the social advantage of conversion already secured over the decades and being reminded of social roots which urban Christians would like to forget. The rural Christians, on the other hand, have used SEBC benefits to their maximum, whenever they could, since then. In Bhalej there are only two cases of Christians having availed themselves of the SEBC provision for jobs, one for a bus driver's job and another for a teacher's job. On this they are very clear that they have simply claimed their constitutional rights without compromising their faith or their religious identity.

There is a diminishing amount of interaction in food, drink, social visits and marital relations between Christian Dalits and Hindu Dalits in the villages, although there is a noticeable tendency to be exclusive on the part of the city Christians. In the case of the city Christians, religious identity takes precedence over caste identity, while in the villages caste and religious identities compete with one other. This is quite in keeping with different prevailing milieus. In the perception of the rural Christians as well as Hindu Dalits, the Christians in the villages were economically poorer prior to their conversion than were Hindu Dalits. Some high caste people in Bhalej corroborate this perception, although a large number of them say that the present condition of both groups in the village is the same. Similarly, a large majority of the non-Dalits in the village perceive both Christian and Hindu Dalits to be equal in social status; however, some do rank Christians higher. In the cities the Christians are perceived to be higher than the Hindu Dalits and non-Dalits have greater interaction with the Christians than with the Hindu Dalits. The rules of avoidance in food and drink persist, but with less severity in cities. The Dalits lower than Vankars in the untouchable caste hierarchy find no different behavioural responses from Christian and Hindu Vankars in rural as well as urban areas. Christian converts want to be equal to those above them, but do not easily accept those below them as equal.

As far as political participation, consciousness and leadership are concerned, in villages as well as in cities, the non-Dalits perceive that both Hindu and Christian Dalits display a lack of confidence and will power. The Christian Dalits find solace and security more in their parish units and depend more on pastors and priests than on the dominant castes. Many people perceive a number of cultural traits such as obedience, good manners, sociability, etc. to be specific to Christians. These pertain to the individual ethics propagated by the normative order of Christianity. However, in the social aspects, such as fighting for one's rights and for justice, Christians are as docile as Hindu Dalits. This could be explained in terms of regional cultural specificity. Generally in Gujarat there has been a pervasive passivist ideology as a result of the prolonged hegemony of business communities, whether Jain or Hindu.

Conversion to Christianity has resulted in the discontinuance of certain cultural practices by the converts, while some practices have continued. Very generally, the Christians have stopped child marriages and in this the role of the missionaries is quite noticeable. In fact, the boys and girls, in a majority of cases, exercise their choice in the selection of their mates. Apart from traditional endogamous caste and marriage circles, the Christian Dalits now also have religious circles within which they marry. The inter-denominational and inter-religious marriages are performed both civilly as well as religiously. Bride price has persisted in the villages despite missionary sanctions. This is so because parents now spend more on their daughters' education. In several cases older religious personnel such as *turi* (bard of Dalits), *garoda* (priest of Dalits), and *sadhu* (religious mendicant) still visit the Christians. The latter oblige them with gifts of cash and kind as an act of piety, not out of religious conviction. While a majority of Christians approach doctors for their health requirements, some continue to resort to faith healers of various kinds. They go to the *bhuva* (spirit-medium), *faqir* and Christian priest in their distress as well as promise and make votive offerings. Although the majority make these vows and offerings to Christ, Mary and Christian saints, there are Christians who make them to Shitala Mata, Bhavani Mata, and Imambaba Pir. A majority of Christians have stopped believing in ghosts, spirits and witchcraft and wearing chanted strings, but they continue to perform housewarming rituals. However, for them the Christian priest performs the ritual. Some Christians take an interest in such Hindu festivals as Diwali, Holi and Rakshabandan. Such practices lead us to ask the question about the extent to which Hindu cosmological categories of time, space and the supernatural have been displaced by Christian categories. There are some indications that they have. The practice of Christian rituals, the reading of Christian scriptures, daily prayer, active participation in Christian associations and activities, have all been vigorous and strong. This is clearly the case with the Bhalej congregations, as they are supported by long historical traditions as well as by active priests who live amongst them.

Overall our study does not record radical change among converts, even though change has definitely affected their worldview. For one, the Dalits of different castes are fairly homogenous and hence are exposed to more or less similar forces and processes. Secondly, those Christians who educated themselves and diversified their occupations have migrated to cities, leaving the poorer ones behind in the villages. Thirdly, in the post-Independence scenario the converts were deprived of Scheduled Caste benefits, while the Hindu Dalits were able to get them and offset the earlier gains in class status which the converts had made.

Several factors hinder the pace of change, if not the change itself, in a typical Indian environment. Caste still happens to be one major factor. All efforts to get away from the caste system have ended up by creating new castes or caste-like structures within the new set-up. Nearly all religions in India—Jainism, Buddhism, Islam, Sikhism, and Christianity—despite a declared non-belief in caste, have caste-like structures. The power of caste ideology is all-pervasive. There are records that a few Chamars accepted Christianity along with Vankars in Kheda district, but nearly all Chamar converts have reverted back to Hinduism, mainly because the Vankars would not accept them on equal footing in food, drink and marriage, although this has not been the case in Bhalej. Christian Dalits seek equality with those higher than themselves but are reluctant to concede it to those below them. Caste has also an economic dimension. Many of the village Dalits have been and still are agricultural labourers. They cannot hope for occupational diversification easily except through migration to cities. Change of religion, unless accompanied by economic freedom, often has left the Dalits in the same place. Without economic transformation the Dalits, whether Christian or Hindu, can have little hope of change. Although "caste" is fast losing its operational value in the cities, it still continues to be a centrally important factor in rural social stratification.

Our reading is that the Christianization of Dalits has helped them in their self-esteem and to a certain degree in the process of upward mobility. From a historical perspective, initially the missionaries came as, and might have appeared as, liberators to the Dalits. Christian missionaries questioned and challenged some aspects of the established order such as social discrimination and were able to stir the imagination of some Dalits by offering the hope of an alternative egalitarian social order under a Christian dispensation. However, in practice the missionaries were so obsessed with the salvation of souls that the social and economic betterment of converts remained a concern of secondary importance to them. The converts, on the other hand, were basically looking for liberation from social and economic degradation (The Bhalej experience, it must be pointed out, is an exception to that general rule, as the early missionaries tried their utmost to buy land and make community members economically self-sufficient). Even when the missionaries launched educational and health programmes, these were viewed by Hindus mainly as vehicles for attracting people to the Christian religion. The end result has been a curious blend of individualistic, salvation-oriented religiosity inculcated by missionaries and some economic and cultural changes expected by the converts. Some of the converts, who educated themselves and diversified their occupations, have been able to realize their expectations and have risen in the social and economic scale. There is also the presence of a genuine Christian religiosity among many of them.

The masses of Dalit converts left behind in the villages have also not remained untouched by the gains accruing from the change in their faith. Their experience shows that the upward mobility of Dalits of all denominations does not lie only in individual morality emanating from their respective religions but in common struggles waged on the socio-political front. As far as Christianization is concerned, we may add that in place of individual morality, social ethics with libertarian ideals of liberty, equality and fraternity may be given more prominence. One could also argue that these ideals can only be achieved by united struggles of all oppressed groups in which Christian Dalits need to take an active political part. What appears on the surface is that an overemphasis upon individual morality advocated by Christianity has contributed somewhat negatively to the converts in India generally. It has, by and large, led to the further domestication of an already docile lowest stratum of society. The political consciousness of Christians generally is very low if not altogether zero. They meekly accept whatever is offered or not offered to them by various state, social or political agencies. Their resistance to violation of their basic human rights has been blunted by missionary domestication.

In concluding these observations on the Bhalej experience of a century old Christian experiment, we are impressed by the optimism exuded by the majority of the community members. Bhalej Christians feel proud of their destiny, even while they would like to forget their past. The developments of the last few years have given them new hope of a forward march with their faith in Christ. They are equally proud of their Christian identity. This is very largely due to a strong historical legacy backed by constantly encouraging pastors and the existence of permanent church buildings. Even though all have not uniformly prospered materially, their faith has not been shaken as they have also started looking at social disparities in socio-political terms. The community members who moved out and have scaled economic as well as social heights through education and/or entrepreneurship have been taken as sources of inspiration rather than as butts of jealousy.

References

A. Interviews with Captain Arvind Christian (Salvation Army), Rev. Santray Philip (CNI), Father Mickey (Roman Catholic), Sylvester Isaac, Zubaidabibi Sayyid, Jasbhai Mangalbhai Patel and several Christians of Bhalej held between September 1998 and October 2000.

B. Books

1. Boyd, Robin H. S., *A Church History of Gujarat*, Madras, 1981.

2. Enthoven, R. E., *Castes and Tribes of Bombay*, 3 vols., Bombay, 1922.

3. Frykenberg, R. E., "On the Study of Conversion Movements: A Review Article and a Theoretical Note", *Indian Economic and Social History Review*, 17,1 (1980), 121-38.

4. Government of Gujarat, *Bharatni Vasti Ganatri 1991: Jilah Vasti Ganatri Pustika: Kheda Jillo.*

5. Israel, Domnik D., A Missiological Evaluation of the Methodist Church in Gujarat during the period of 1921-1987, MTM Diss., Michigan: UMI, 1989.

6. Joseph, Mercy, The Role of Christian Missionaries in Central Gujarat during the Nineteenth Century, M.Phil. Diss., M. S. University of Baroda, 1997.

7. Lobo, Lancy, Religious Conversion and Social Mobility (A Case Study of the Vankars in Central Gujarat), Centre for Social Studies, Surat, 1991 (Mimeo).

8. Oddie, G. A., *Religion in South Asia: Religious Conversion and Revival Movements in South Asia in Medieval and Modern Times,* New Delhi, 1977.

9. Shah, Ghanshyam, "Anti-Untouchability Movements" in I.P. Desai (ed.), *Caste, Caste Conflicts and Reservation*, Delhi, 1985.

10. Smith, Solveig, *By Love Compelled: The Story of 100 Years of the Salvation Army in India and adjacent Countries*, London, 1981.

11. Suria, Carlos, *History of the Catholic Church in Gujarat*, Anand, 1990.

CHAPTER 6

THE PEOPLE WHO BELIEVE THAT GOD IS FAITHFUL: THE STORY OF THE PEOPLE OF THE TURKMAN DARWAZAH (HOLY TRINITY CHURCH), DELHI

Monodeep Daniel

Turkman Gate is named after the Turkish dynasty of Qutab-ud-din whose son Illtumish occupied the throne of Delhi from 1211 to 1236 AD.[1] Once at the southern edge of the walled city of Delhi about a kilometre west of the Yamuna river, Turkman Gate now is a major corridor connecting Daryaganj, the Old Delhi city centre, to Connaught Place, the city centre for New Delhi. Flanked on one side by the high rising buildings of the stock exchange, banks, offices of various companies and business firms, and on the other by Haz Manzil, the Christian *basti* is now completely hidden from view.

A warm acceptance of my invitation by Sri Hansraj Bhardwaj, former Law Minister in the Congress government and now a member of the Rajya Sabha, surprised me a little because normally invitations to Church functions were politely declined by Members of Parliament in my previous pastorate. Sri Bhardwaj was the Chief Guest for the Church's annual fete in 1998. In his speech on that day he described the Christian *basti* of Turkman Gate as an "island of peace." He movingly recalled the love he had received from the people there during the trying period of 1977-78 when Mrs. Indira Gandhi had placed him in that area to work for the Congress Party. Visiting house to house he often faced hostility and ridicule from

---

[1] *Gazetteer of India: Delhi,* Delhi: Delhi Administration, 1996, 47.

both the Muslim and the Hindu sections. Tired and frustrated, he would enter the Christian *basti* where a *charpai* would be provided and tea served. Old and young would sit and talk with him. Since then the Turkman Gate Christian community has had a special place in his heart. "This Church has made all the difference in the lives of this people," he said pointing to the beautiful Byzantine church building. This remark had a deeper significance for me. It was pointing to the faith and conviction of the people which this building represented. These people were once leather workers living in the Daryaganj and Mirkhanganj area of the walled city of Old Delhi behind the Turkman Gate, demeaningly called "Chamars" by caste Hindus. The story I write in the pages that follow is of these people who believed that God remains faithful to His promise.

THEIR BEGINNING AS A CHRISTIAN PEOPLE 1859-1899

The Christian mission in Delhi was completely destroyed in May 1857. In 1859 the leather-workers from a neighbouring village of Shahdara contacted the Anglican missionary, Mr. Skelton, through the S. P. G. catechist, Heera Lal, to seek Christian instruction.[2] In this village only five heads of families showed an interest in Christianity but he addressed an assembly of 100 people. Later that year five people received baptism from the Baptists.[3] Shahdara was not the only place where leather-workers were interested in Christianity. There was also a response from the Purana Quila and Southeastern Quarter within the city walls. Worship was soon held on weekdays in houses in the Delhi Gate area. From August 1860 leather-workers in the city were in contact with Rev. Robert Winter, a Society for the Propagation of the Gospel (S. P. G.) missionary whose initial efforts had been devoted to establishing St. Stephens' High School as well as its branches in various *bastis*. [4]

---

[2] Canon Skelton, "The Revival of the Delhi Mission after the Mutiny," *Delhi Mission News* (April 1896), 7.

[3] *Delhi Mission News* (July 1896), 12.

[4] *Ibid.* (October 1896), 9-10.

In 1878 Edward Bickersteth wrote that Mr. Winter had baptized 300 to 400 people of Chamar origin who had been "largely influenced by means of these schools and the services connected with them."[5] Later in 1884, Mr. Lefroy further explained that large numbers had converted during the famine of 1877-78.[6] Besides the influence of Christianity in the schools and the relief services rendered during the 1877-78 famine, the bazaar (market) preaching also had its influence. It was, as missionary contemporaries said, "casting bread upon the waters." As a result, communities oppressed by caste practices became aware of an alternative socio-religious system which promised liberation and equality. Hence the Chamars' embracing of Christian faith was primarily guided by the aim of improving their social conditions. They never took the religious and spiritual aspects of Christianity with due seriousness. Lefroy argued that the 800 leather-workers converted were "Christians in nothing but name, yet in name Christians," and therefore it was not morally justifiable for the Cambridge Mission to Delhi to decline to assist Mr. Winter "in the tremendously difficult task that lay before him ... of raising the whole spiritual position of these poor people."[7]

It is interesting to note that the Cambridge Mission to Delhi fathers related to the S. P. G. were constantly justifying their work among the Delhi leather-workers. For example, Mr. Bickersteth began writing a letter to Canon Westcott by stating that "Our special duty as a mission is to endeavour to reach the higher classes," but towards the end of the letter he said,

> The care of the small Christian congregations gathered by Mr. Winter during recent years from among the despised Hindoo caste of leather-workers, did not come within the plan of the Cambridge Mission as it was originally drawn. The work, however, itself increased so largely, as to be altogether beyond the activity of

[5] Cambridge Mission to Delhi, *Occasional Papers* (October 16, 1878), 13.

[6] G. A. Lefroy, *The Leather-workers of Daryaganj,* Cambridge Mission to Delhi Occasional Papers, 1884, 4.

[7] *Ibid.,* 5.

any one man, even that of the founder of the mission among these people, to overtake. We, therefore, felt justified in undertaking that part of the work which we have in hand, about half of the whole.[8]

This indicates that not all were happy with their work among the lowly and poor leather-workers. Meanwhile S. P. G. mission workers continued to build contacts and rapport with Hindus and Muslims.

One of the issues faced by the missionaries in dealing with their Chamar converts was whether to leave the new converts in their own *biradari* (caste brotherhood) "to be a light to their own world" or to segregate them in a separate compound where "they would be free to carry on their own trade under precisely the old conditions." Lefroy preferred the second option of segregation over and against Winter's insistence on the first.[9] He therefore arranged to build a little square of eight houses in Daryaganj and offered to rent one to any Christian who agreed to three conditions: 1) to observe Sunday as a day of rest; 2) to use Christian rites exclusively at times of birth, marriage and death; and 3) to abstain from the use of *charas* (a drug with properties similar to opium).[10] Lefroy reported that there was "a continual bickering between the different families as to what was and what was not consistent with their new and more distinctly Christian attitude." He noted with interest that "each member being inclined to be very liberal in the concessions which he made to himself and the favour with which he regarded the invitations of his own friends, but very much the reverse where his neighbour was concerned, and this quarrelling increased so much as to threaten the very life of this little community."[11]

To resolve this issue, a *panchayat* meeting was convened of all those Chamars living in the city and its suburbs. The *panchayat* was formed by the 250 representatives of each clan in a set of 52

[8] A Letter to Canon Wescott by Revd E. Bickersteth, Sept. 1 1881,Cambridge Mission to Delhi Occassional Papers, 2 & 7.

[9] G. A. Lefroy, *The Leather-workers of Daryaganj*, 8-10.

[10] *Ibid.*, 11.

[11] *Ibid.*

villages (*Bawani*). The Daryaganj Christian *basti* was chosen for
the convocation which took place on a summer night in 1884. The
meeting commenced at midnight. The set purpose of the meeting
for the converts was to force a choice between a Christian way of
life and that of the Chamar *biradari*. Mission personnel were present
with the converts sitting a little apart from the rest. Converts who
had opposed this convocation and had decided to stay aloof were
summoned as well.

The meeting was started by the catechist, then taken over by
the *Chaudri* and other Christian men who explained that they would
no longer continue with the brotherhood of leather-workers but
would be glad to reckon many individuals among them as personal
friends. All went smoothly until the nomination of the next Chaudri
by the Chaudri who had just resigned because of his conversion to
Christianity. His nominee was his nephew who was not a Christian.
This was rejected, an indication of the strong undercurrent of
opposition to Christianity. The Chamars' aim was to "sift out the
Christians." This was to be done by setting a pot of Ganges water
in the midst of the meeting and calling on those supposed to be
Christian to either raise it to their foreheads as a sign of worship
or bear ejection from the caste. The problems of naming the
Christians and procuring the Ganges water were sorted out. Each
headman would name those from his jurisdiction who were to raise
Ganges water and the Ganges water was quickly procured by a
boy who was seen to go in the direction of the nearest well!

Accordingly, the first five names called were men of "weak
character, low esteem and poor position." They obeyed the
summons and raised the water to their heads. Then came the turn
of a young man, sitting with a small group whose decision to remain
faithful to Jesus Christ proved to be the turning point of the night's
business. Chaudhri Ghisa[12] was a well-to-do active man, much
respected by all the Christians and Chamars alike, already a Chaudri
in his own right and with the prospect of a second Chaudriship

---

[12] The name of this young man does not appear in the written records
of this event, but is remembered in the community as Chaudhri Ghisa.

from his father if he reverted from Christianity. Lefroy wrote that "it was really a moment not to be soon forgotten . . . as the father stooped down and looked his son full in the face for a few moments. No word was exchanged. Then: 'What are you doing here?' 'In my place with the Christians.' 'Come with me at once.' 'I can't.' 'Take up the Ganges water.' 'Never.' That was all; and then, with a look of the deepest resentment, the father withdrew. Behind him all the rest of his clan, of which he was by his old right Chaudri, stood firm. By 7:30 in the morning the meeting ended and they adjourned, with all Christians present, to the little chapel nearby for a short service."[13] It was found that out of 25 heads of families only five had lapsed.[14]

After this kind of test had been applied in many districts, one last opportunity was granted to all recalcitrants before a final sentence of excommunication was passed upon them. This was done at a large *Panchayat* meeting held in the S. P. G. compound on 25th May 1887.[15] Of the 990 people whose status was doubtful, 290 were excommunicated from the church that night. Under the guidance of Bishop French three minimum conditions were laid down for church membership: 1) that all Christians with unbaptized children bring them for baptism and put their wives under instruction with a view to baptism; 2) that they form betrothals for their children only among Christians; and 3) that they attend no fairs or ceremonies which involved idolatrous practices.[16]

Apart from the conversion of the Chamars in the first place, this "sifting out" was the main event of the period. It should also be noted that famine struck once again in 1897-98. The Christian shoemakers suffered like the rest of the poor people. The mission organized relief work for them, as they were hit exceptionally hard; they were unable to buy sufficient food because there were hardly

---

[13] This description of the proceedings of the *Panchayat* meeting follows that given by Lefroy, who was present, in *ibid.*, 14-21.

[14] Short Papers of the S. P. G. and C. M. D. No. 9 (1902), 2.

[15] *Ibid.*, 9.

[16] *The Story of the Delhi Mission*, second edition; London: Society for the Propagation of the Gospel in Foreign Parts, 1917, 50-51.

any sales of their shoes in the market. The Mission helped them by subsidizing their work on every pair of shoes they made.[17]

LEARNING TO BE A CHURCH
1900-1947

The twentieth century commenced with an event which, though localized in nature, reflected the socio-economic condition of the shoemakers. In July 1902 the Christian shoemakers, like the rest of their *biradari,* suffered economically from a lock-out by *beoparis* (middle-men). This happened due to a row between a *beopari* and a shoemaker who alleged that he had been grievously wronged. The legal decision of the court had no effect on the *beoparis* and they took action of their own lines. They stopped all business dealings with shoemakers. This caused a complete stand-still in the trade. The shoemakers decided not to give in to this and no sooner did the lock-out end, than a shoemakers' strike began. The Christian shoemakers affected by the cessation of business approached the Mission to intervene. The *beoparis* were also eager to reconcile, but this attempt was unsuccessful. "Salvation came from an unlooked for quarter." The *sahukars* (money lenders who loaned money to shoemakers on a large scale for marriages and trade), realized that if the situation continued they would lose all hopes of collecting both interest and capital on their loans. As a result of the *sahukars'* intervention, the conflict was resolved, though it was noted to be nothing less than a farce. During these proceedings the *beoparis* spoke highly of the Christian shoemakers as being honest and hard working.[18]

In describing this conflict, Allnutt noted with concern the cycle of socio-economic exploitation to which the Christian and other shoemakers were subject. The shoemakers were totally dependent on the *beoparis* for securing the money needed for making shoes.

[17] "From our Delhi Correspondent," *Delhi Mission News* (January 1897), 3-4.

[18] S. S. Allnutt, "A Lock-out and Strike in Delhi," *Delhi Mission News* (January 1902), 55-56.

Often the *beoparis* received the shoes and then threw them inside a stock-room while they bargained with the helpless vendor. Sometimes the shoemakers were permanently shackled in debt because they spent the money advanced for production on gambling and drinking so that the lender had little chance to recover his loan. "But the profits of the 'Beoparis' are so great and their hold over the chamars so tight that they willingly put up with these losses." These *beoparis* were Muslims; Hindus considered leather work to be unclean and kept aloof from the manufacturing process, but did wear leather shoes nonetheless. The Christian shoemakers, like the rest, were also victims of this caste stigma, in spite of their conversion, and remained poor.[19]

For the Christian shoemakers living under such social conditions, the erection of The Holy Trinity Church was an important landmark in their community life. It was built in memory of Alexander Charles Maitland, an S. P. G. missionary (1853-1894) who had left Rs. 10,000 "for the purpose of building a church in a distant quarter of the city."[20] The church building designed by Revd A. Coore was to be a beautiful Byzantine structure with domes all around and one at the centre of the roof. The site, originally at Ajmeri Gate, was shifted to Turkman Gate due to Government plans for laying railway tracks through that area. The present site was near the Christian *basti* and therefore suitable for building the church. It was hoped that the Muslim-owned property in front of the church would also be bought to give a frontage on the main road and an open space in front of the Church.[21] This happened only later. The church was consecrated on 7th November 1905 by Bishop Lefroy. Among the signatories of the petition to the bishop for the consecration of the church were Messers Abdul Hameed, Mukkha, Munna Lal, Paltu and Kaisariya from the Christian shoemakers community. Bishop Lefroy preached on the day of

[19] *Ibid.*

[20] S. S. Allnutt, "Head of the Mission's Page," *Delhi Mission News* (April 1900), 113.

[21] S. S. Allnutt, "Head of the Mission's Page," *Delhi Mission News* (July 1902), 78.

consecration from Eph. 5:20 which is relevant even now for the *basti.*[22]

> Look, therefore carefully how ye walk not as unwise, but as wise, redeeming the time because the days are evil. Wherefore, be ye not foolish but understand what the will of the Lord is. And be not drunken with wine, wherein is riot, but be filled with the spirit, speaking one to another in Psalms and Hymns and spiritual songs, singing and making melody with your heart to the Lord; giving thanks always for all things in the name of our Lord Jesus Christ to God, even the Father.

The erection of this church building helped to give the people in the *basti* a distinct identity amidst the dominating Muslim and Hindu population. The church building was large, very attractive, and the common property of all the Christian people. Common public worship there most probably contributed to bringing about social consolidation. This building was a community possession and many visitors came to see it. For instance, they welcomed foreign delegates who came to attend the Delhi Assembly of the World Council of Churches in 1961 and the visit of the Archbishop of Canterbury and Mrs. Ramsey was a pleasant surprise for the people.[23] This undoubtedly gave a boost to their social standing. From being marginalized, they had become a centre of attraction. This distinct and new identity became the inner force enabling them to climb the social ladder of progress. A place like Delhi provided ample opportunity for them to do this. Perhaps this is what was in Mr. Bhardwaj's mind when he referred to the Church building as the one thing which made all the difference to the people's life.

In the years following World War I the numerical growth of the community through conversion slowed down. During the civil disobedience movement preaching in the bazaars and Bickersteth Hall was halted as it was "bound to . . . create an unfavourable

---

[22] "Consecration of Three Churches," *Delhi Mission News* (January 1906), 107-108; Report of the Year 1905 of the Society for the Propagation of the Gospel in Foreign Parts, 85-86.

[23] "Delhi in 1961," The Annual Report of the Diocese of Delhi and Cambridge Mission to Delhi, 18.

atmosphere for the reception of the Gospel message."[24] In addition, a number of the more upward mobile families at Turkman Gate preferred to move on to St. Stephen's Church and so deprived the Turkman Gate parish of their moral and financial help. This move was a result of Holy Trinity being seen as a "caste church."[25] Even today the elderly remember Holy Trinity being called as *"Chamaro ka Girja."* Victimized by poverty and caste, the people got new hope from Hugh Basil King, an S.P.G. and Cambridge Mission to Delhi missionary who brought fresh vision to the church.[26] The Christian people of Turkman Gate under his leadership began to learn self-dependency. They benefited greatly from the immense building work which he undertook in the church compound. In 1934 the Turkman Gate area was greatly improved by demolitions and three alms-houses were built there for widows.[27] In 1935 two small houses were purchased in front of the church; these were then demolished to make way for a front road.[28] In 1936 the Turkman Gate premises were extended by buying one more house and Bari Basti in Daryaganj was rebuilt with the money received after selling Choti Basti. Some families from Choti Basti were shifted to the Turkman Gate premises. The Municipal Committee also acquired the land between Turkman Gate and New Delhi for development; a number of shoemakers had to be helped to get a fair settlement because they were illiterate and unfamiliar with the legalities involved.[29]

However, some serious problems remained. One was prostitution, which is not surprising when one keeps in view the

[24] B. H. King writing in The S. P. G. and Cambridge Mission to Delhi 53rd Report (1930), 5 & 16.

[25] The S. P. G. and Cambridge Mission to Delhi 52nd Report (1929), 18.

[26] *Ibid.*, 6.

[27] The S. P. G. and Cambridge Mission to Delhi 57th Report (1934), 7.

[28] The S. P. G. and Cambridge Mission to Delhi 58th Report (1935), 5.

[29] The S. P. G. and Cambridge Mission to Delhi 60th Report (1937), 10.

poverty and low self-esteem of the people. Another problem was the gradual decay of shoe-making as a home industry due to the fall in demand in the market. The intervention of YWCA social workers and other economic alleviation programmes did not bring about significant changes and the 1930s were particularly difficult years for the people.[30] For example, in 1934 an attempt was made to start a savings bank for all shoemakers, but this did not work well. Slightly more successful was rug weaving taught to the people by missionaries in 1936-37.[31] In 1938 several young men and boys were reported to be benefiting and the quality of production was remarkable.[32]

An important step towards the future development of the community was the creation of the Holy Trinity Primary School in 1940. Up to that time education had not been a priority for the people; even though primary education was free and compulsory for Delhi boys, the children of the parish were admitted to schools only at 8 years of age.[33] Since parish children did not benefit much from the private and municipal schools, Revd J. H. Bishop, then vicar of Holy Trinity Church, moved the Mission Council to permit him to start a primary school. The school was started on 1st April 1940 and received recognition as a grant-in-aid school in March 1944. That generation of parish children was all educated in that school. The hope of having the entire community become literate was also realized in the later years.[34] Some children now are studying in the most prestigious schools in the city, including St. Stephen's College.

---

[30] Miss Gould in The S. P. G. and Cambridge Mission to Delhi 61st Report (1938), 9.

[31] Mr. King in The S. P. G. and Cambridge Mission to Delhi 60th Report (1937), 10.

[32] Miss Gould in The S. P. G. and Cambridge Mission to Delhi 61st Report (1938), 9.

[33] A. E. Adolphus in *Delhi Quarterly Paper* (October 1950), 40.

[34] Report of the Diocese of Delhi and Cambridge Mission to Delhi (1948), 27.

The religious life of this Christian shoemakers community was developed around the Church Liturgical Cycle of Christmas, Easter, Pentecost and Ascension which made a deep impact on their minds. The centre of celebration was the Holy Trinity Church in Turkman Gate. The language of the liturgy was Urdu. People came from Ajmere Gate, Ganj Mirkhan, Delhi Gate, Daryaganj and Kalan Masjid. Their social life was also organized around their church, with a central *panchayat* (parish council) and sub-*panchayats*. At that time the status of Delhi within the Anglican Communion was that of a Province under the Bishopric of Lahore. In April 1944 the S.P.G. and Cambridge Mission to Delhi work was merged into the Archdeaconry of Delhi under Archdeacon (later Bishop) A. N. Mukerjee. In those years Revd Arthur Adolphus was the parish priest of the Holy Trinity Church. The people learned two significant things from him. First, they learned to be a Church, which meant learning the duty and privilege of giving. In 1944 they gave Rs. 385 for missionary work. This change was remarkable, as just a year earlier people expected the mission to do everything for them. Secondly, they learned the importance of education. Eighty children were reported to be in the primary school and they needed a new building.[35]

Three months prior to the independence of India, on 21st April 1947, Delhi was upgraded to a Diocese and A. N. Mukerjee was enthroned as its first bishop. On the whole the shoemakers community had never actively participated in the freedom struggle. They, however, were affected by the political upheavals when their Muslim neighbours began to leave for Pakistan. They saw houses left empty and abandoned. It was not long before Punjabi Hindus and Sikhs arrived from Pakistan. They were rehabilitated in those vacant houses and the *basti* Christians had to reckon with the arrival of new neighbours. The Christians who were accustomed to the Delhi Muslims were unable to appreciate the newly arrived Punjabis. In fact, they blamed the Punjabis for heightening sexual promiscuity in the neighbourhood.

[35] Report of the Archdeaconary of Delhi and Cambridge Mission to Delhi (1944), 12.

In August and September 1947 Hindu-Muslim riots broke out throughout Delhi. One or two Christians were reported to be mistaken for Muslims and killed; several lost property because of looting, but the urban Christians faced no antagonism. In the rural districts, however, Hindus threatened the small low-caste Christian congregations with death unless they reverted to Hinduism. Bishop Mukerjee wrote in November 1947 that "In the districts, some of our people through terrible pressure and fear have broken down. It is a sad story; ...We have to rebuild the Church with those who have been faithful, and by a sifting process reclaim those who have remained true in heart, but through fear have lapsed."[36] Sadly, this story was true also for Holy Trinity Parish. Many lapsed in Ganj Mirkhan. However, the people living in the Christian *basti*, church compound, and Kings Compound in Turkman Gate, which are within the precincts of the Church, remained faithful. So also did many others outside as well as those in Daryaganj Bari Basti. This suggests that many in the shoemaker community, in their search for liberation and protection, had aligned themselves with socially and politically dominant British missionaries. However, once British rule ended and the prospects of continued liberation and protection seemed bleak, there were those who either considered it prudent to revert back to their former religion or did so under pressure.

A CHANGING CHURCH IN
A CHANGING NEIGHBOURHOOD
1950-2000

In the years following Independence Delhi both expanded and became more crowded. Churches that once were rural parishes were swallowed up in urban expansion; those that had proper church buildings survived but others did not. With a shortage of both churches and clergy within the Delhi diocese, the Holy Trinity Church was placed directly under the bishop's charge. Since then

---

[36] Report for the Year 1947 of the Diocese of Delhi and Cambridge Mission to Delhi, 11.

all of its pastors have been full-time, although some, such as those who were members of the Cambridge Mission to Delhi (now the Brotherhood of the Ascended Christ), have had other responsibilities as well. The congregation was not affected by the church union in 1970 when the Anglicans joined the Church of North India; the members continue to prefer the Anglo-Catholic ritualism inherited from their Anglican past in their liturgical life. Today Holy Trinity is considered one of the major churches of the Delhi Diocese of the Church of North India; it plays an active role in the life and work of the diocese.

Three important developments affecting the city at large have had an impact upon the Turkman Gate *basti*. The first of these was overcrowding. The following description, published in 1961, describes the problem.

> The *basti* consists of eighteen residential quarters, each with one room and a small verandah, surrounding a common courtyard. . . . At one end of the courtyard is a set of public latrines. Water for all the homes is obtained from a municipal tap just outside the *basti* wall. Some tenants have installed electrical connections at their own expense while others use oil lamps. The community includes 15 families and 6 widows, a total of 90 people crowded into a human rabbit warren. It should be noted that the occupants of the *basti* regard their situation as being better than that of most Christians living in adjoining areas of the city. Their quarters, though small, are well-built and rents are low. They are protected from non-Christian influences and community discipline on the whole is good.[37]

The Delhi government introduced slum improvement plans, providing an underground drainage system, fresh water supply, paved roads, and electricity. The Turkman Gate compound benefited from these developments and the residents made major improvements in their homes. Today most of the houses are double-storeyed and made with brick and cement, but overcrowding remains a serious problem. The increase in population has had

---

[37] James P. Alter and Herbert Jai Singh, *The Church in Delhi*, Lucknow: National Christian Council of India, 1961, 87.

political consequences. Today the *basti* is a stronghold of the Congress Party which is eager to keep their votes and the people there are eager to have its protection.

The second development is the dispersal of the Church's membership. Not all the members live in or near the Turkman Gate compound. For example, 32 of the 52 present members of the Church's Youth Committee do live in Turkman Gate and another six live at the Christian compound in Daryaganj. Thus, while the Church continues to draw a solid core of its membership from its traditional *basti* bases, one can see signs of outward migration of people who yet remain loyal to the Holy Trinity Church.

A third change is represented by the social mobility of the members. This has been a long term process, earlier signs of which are apparent in the entries in the Church marriage register from 1907-1946 given in Appendix I. While shoe-making was the traditional occupation of all the original members of the *basti*, one can see that marriages of shoemakers remained quite steady up through 1932 but afterwards only three occurred. Meanwhile marriages among people in other occupations, especially teaching and skilled labour, began to increase markedly. This trend included women (marked F) as well as men. The present youth committee consists mostly of students, but those who are employed work in a variety of occupations. Today not a single resident of the Turkman Gate *basti* or member of the Holy Trinity Church is engaged in shoe-making. One of the most significant consequences of this occupational mobility has been the emergence of economic classes within the church and *basti* among what had once been a homogenous community.

These social changes have made their impact upon the life of the church itself. In 1950 a Mother's Union was formed which drew educated women into its membership and helped them become pillars of the church. In February 1955 the church celebrated its Jubilee for a whole week. The organizing capabilities of the people became apparent, in contrast to the more dependent behaviour of previous generations. Important people visited the church, including Lady Clutterbuck, wife of the British High Commissioner. Two

thousand people gathered for the Jubilee procession from Daryaganj
to Turkman Gate where a thanksgiving service was held and 1600
people enjoyed a community dinner.[38] Since then the church has
contributed two members to the priesthood, Rajinder Kumar Daniel
and George Lazar.[39] It has also faced very aggressive recruitment
efforts of Pentecostals, Jehovah's Witnesses, Full Gospel Chapel,
and Seventh Day Adventists. Later a sect called "Believers" made
some inroads, calling into question the practice of infant baptism
and leading some to undergo a "second baptism" by immersion.[40]
Most recently some members have been attracted to the "End Time
Believers" who do not believe in the Trinity and baptize only in
the name of Jesus. These sects seem to attract those who, over a
period of time, have felt that their dignity and self-esteem have
been injured either by acts of their own or by the insults of others.

   Today there are 230 families enrolled as contributing members
of the Holy Trinity Church. They are descendants of those early
families who remained faithful to Christ. There have been marriage
alliances among them as well as with other Dalit Christian families
from other parts of Delhi or from the Punjab. Some of the residents
have married Hindus or Muslims, but no Christian families from
non-Chamar backgrounds have moved into the *basti*. The
relationship of the Turkman Gate Christians with the Chamar
biradari, however, has not been strong. In fact, the gate between
the Turkman Gate compound and the *biradari* quarters outside
remains locked and no one knows where the key is! Although some
families do have non-Christian relatives just outside the church
compound, social contacts are minimal. Occasionally, some women
from the *biradari* quarters do attend church services. The recent
persecution of Christians in the Dangs area of Gujarat state has
given the community a sense of insecurity. Some of its leaders
have sought police protection, while others sought a stronger
relationship with Muslims and even helped to organize a Minority

---

[38] Delhi in 1955: The Annual Report of the Diocese of Delhi, 17;
discussions with members.
[39] Delhi in 1963, 9.
[40] Delhi in 1950, 17-18; Delhi in 1952, 19.

Secular Front which was responsible for the demonstration on the road in front of the *basti* and the burning of Mr. Advani's effigy in public view. An overall view of its past history indicates that in the final analysis this church has survived because its members believe that God is faithful.

APPENDIX-I

Year of Registry	Number of Marriage	Shoe-making	Domestic	Other
1907	4	1	1	cook clerk
1908	2	2	-	-
1909	1	1	-	-
1910	2	1	-	(in band) lancenaik
1911	3	3	-	-
1912	1	1	-	-
1914	1	1	-	-
1916	2	1	1	-
1917	1	1	-	-
1918	1	-	-	teacher
1921	5	2	-	2 carpenters teacher
1922	3	2	-	engine driver
1923	2	2	-	-
1924	2	-	-	electrician-tramway carpenter
1925	2	1	-	carpenter
1926	2	-	-	journalist shopkeeper
1927	1	1	-	-
1928	1	1	-	-
1929	3	2	-	clerk(m) health-worker(f)
1930	4	2	-	cook(m) teacher(f) schoolman(m) zamendar(f)
1932	5	2	1	service (m) clerk(m)
1933	4	-	-	carpenter electrician driver teacher

Year of Registry	Number of Marriage	Shoe-making	Domestic	Other
1934	4	-	labourer	peon
				student
				veg. seller
1935	3	-	-	technical-unspecified
1936	3	-	labourer	fitter
				professional-unspecified
1937	7	-	labourer	electrician
				goldsmith
				govt. press printer
				service
				teacher
1938	11	-	-	2 mechanics
				2 compositors
				press
				driver
				business mission-worker
				teacher
				tailor
				dispensary
1939	7	2	1	fitter
				painter
				driver
				carpenter
1940	1	-	-	engine driver
1941	7	-	-	turner
				fitter
				2 motor-drivers
				tailor
				2 service
1942	2	-	-	teacher(m)
				nurse(f)
				clerk

Year of Registry	Number of Marriage	Shoe-making	Domestic	Other
1943	7	-	bearer	fitter wireman-telegraph clerk(m) nurse(f) 2 service clerk
1944	5	1	-	technical- unspecified cook service military nurse(m) nurse(f)
1945	2	-	-	clerk(m) nurse(f) service
1946	6	-	-	fitter painter tailor teacher professional- unspecified

CHAPTER 7

WRITING LOCAL DALIT CHRISTIAN HISTORY

John C. B. Webster

There is at present a growing body of historical writing on the Dalits.[1] There is also a general history as well as a number of regional histories of Dalit Christians.[2] Because this was the first attempt to bring together some essays in local history dealing with Dalit Christians, it turned out to be quite an adventure. There were no clear models to follow and the authors had to rely on some very broad guidelines as well as their own ingenuity when preparing draft chapters. At the seminar where these drafts were presented, a special session was devoted to sharing stories about how the authors went about their research, the practical problems they ran into, and the insights they gained on how to proceed with further research in revising their drafts for publication. The purpose of this chapter is to share some reflections upon the process of doing research on local Dalit Christian history in the hope that others might benefit from our experience.

The great challenge and excitement in local history is to discover how particular face-to-face communities of people actually lived out their lives together. National and regional histories are, of necessity, rather selective and abstracted from local realities since they deal with broader movements, trends and conditions. Those of us who approach local history from regional or national history

---

[1] A survey of books in English on modern Dalit history is found in John C. B. Webster, "Towards Understanding the Modern Dalit Movement," *The Fourth World*, No. 7 (April 1998), 13-36. Several more histories have appeared since that article was published.

[2] These are listed in the bibliography at the end of this article.

are interested to find out how prevailing circumstances and changes affected local communities, if at all; in that sense local history provides an important test of the validity of the generalizations we make about broader developments. On the other hand, those of us who begin with local history and the families who constitute a particular local community may be interested in that community's life and particular issues or how their community has been affected by outside forces, or both. This starting point is specially vital when one is going into the history of one's own local community or of a local community with which one identifies. In all of these chapters the authors have looked at local Dalit Christian communities and congregations in their own right as well as in relationship to some of the more general realities of Dalit Christian life.

Although differing in their approaches, the authors have drawn upon three inter-related types of knowledge in writing the essays that have appeared here. The first is that provided by the source materials they have consulted and referred to in their footnotes and lists of references. These source materials vary considerably, ranging from missionary accounts, to local church registers, to interviews with present members of Dalit congregations. The second type of knowledge is that provided by the changing contexts within which these local histories have unfolded and which in varying ways have shaped those histories. These contexts are in every case multiple. They include, at the very least, the histories of the city or village in which the congregation lives, the broader trends in regional Dalit movements of which they may have been a part, and the church traditions of those missionaries and Indian Christian leaders with whom specific groups of Dalit Christians have become connected. The third type of knowledge is that provided by the historiography of Dalit movements in general, of Dalit Christian movements in particular, or of congregations in general. This type of knowledge provides some of the questions which these historians have used to interrogate their source materials and the contexts they have referred to. Each type of knowledge interacts with the others and contributes to the process of writing the history. For purposes of convenience we will treat them separately.

SOURCE MATERIALS

Writing Dalit history, in whatever form, including Dalit Christian history, requires considerable ingenuity. Dalits, traditionally, have been a non-literate people who have left few sources of their own behind for historians to consult in order to "hear their voice." One pastor did discover some songs composed by early converts in his village, which are still being sung there,[3] but this is the exception rather than the rule. To compound the problem, others have considered Dalits to be so low on the social scale and thus so unimportant as to be hardly worth writing anything about. As a result, literate people who might have written about them have largely ignored them and produced few sources about them. It is at this point, however, that Christian Dalits have had an advantage; once they took an interest in Christianity and went so far as to accept baptism, foreign missionaries and Indian pastors started producing sources about them from which at least portions of their histories can be reconstructed.

In the preceding chapters, the authors have drawn upon a wide variety of source materials which might be simply categorized here at the outset. There are the references to local Dalit churches and communities in the reports, correspondence, and articles written by missionaries and Indian mission workers. Rarely do these references tell a full, ready-made story, but they do provide fragments of different kinds of information, which the historian can put together with other fragments in order to get a picture of the past. There are also the baptismal, marriage and burial registers kept in local churches. Rarely are old minute books to be found and they might tell a great deal more. There is what might be termed archaeological evidence in the form of church buildings, residences

---

[3] John C. B. Webster et al., *From Role to Identity: Dalit Christian Women in Transition*, Delhi: ISPCK, 1997, 58. The pastor was the Rev. D. C. Premraj in Vedal Village in Tamil Nadu.

and inscriptions on them as well as in cemeteries. There is local lore not only about the ancestors but also about the customs, traditions, festivals, and important events in community life which are passed on from one generation to the next. There are present members of the church and community who can be interviewed and whose memories may provide invaluable information. These are the most obvious and most frequently utilized sources, but there are others as well. In one of these studies, the congregation was described briefly in a sociological study carried out forty years ago; the observations provided there are now a useful reference point for understanding the church and community at that point in its history.[4] Land records played an important role in a study prepared for this project but not completed. In that instance, the records were assembled for a court case between Dalit Christian villagers and their former landlord which proved to be a defining event in the history of that particular Dalit Christian community. One cannot dismiss pastoral insight as an important source of understanding; the pastor may be interviewed not merely for memories of specific persons and events but also to gain insight into the changing moods, dynamics, and the often unarticulated or silenced "issues" of the congregation.

While there is much overlap in the ways in which our essayists use these diverse sources, there are also important differences which should be pointed out. P. Dayanandan uses mission sources primarily to provide context, to describe the foundation period of the Andreyapuram community, and to explain why higher education

---

[4] The reference is to the description of the Holy Trinity Church in Delhi in James P. Alter and Herbert Jai Singh, *The Church in Delhi* (Lucknow: Lucknow Publishing, 1961), 86-87. Its history is given here in chapter 6 by Monodeep Daniel. When I was looking for a village in the Punjab to study, I considered using the two villages described in a study belonging to the same series: E. Y. Campbell, *The Church in the Punjab: Some Aspects of its Life and Growth* (Lucknow, Lucknow Publishing House, 1961). However, I found that the villages no longer exist! One had been destroyed in a flood and the other had been swallowed up by the growing city of Jullundur.

as a pathway to upward mobility was effectively blocked for a long time. George Oommen uses them primarily for context and Monodeep Daniel relies on them almost exclusively for the early history of the Dalit Christians at Turkman Gate in Delhi. While these uses may be influenced by what our authors were interested in or by the particular mission sources available to them, these uses also say something important about the sources themselves as well as about the people who produced them. As has been noted elsewhere, in their writings (often for an overseas readership) missionaries involved with Dalit Christians revealed a far greater interest in "the work" than in the people and thus tended to look at the latter through administrative lenses; most often their writings provide only generalized impressions of trends or issues rather than rich descriptive detail about individuals, local communities and congregations.[5] Thus it is often necessary to scan a large quantity of mission sources just to find a few relevant details.

Church registers for baptisms, marriages and burials provide a very rich source of evidence concerning local Dalit Christian history, especially when they contain information about family connections and occupations. George Oommen, Monodeep Daniel, and Godwin Shiri have drawn heavily upon this type of source for evidence of social mobility among members of the congregation across the generations, whereas P. Dayanandan has used these sources to trace the progress of the mass conversion movements and family connections.

The "archaeological" source most frequently referred to is the church building itself. Some describe its style and present condition. Rajkumar Hans and Siddhi Macwan as well as Monodeep Daniel have used inscriptions on or in the church building primarily for dating purposes. In addition, Daniel has also described in some detail the changes which have taken place in the houses of the Christian *basti* around the Holy Trinity Church. These changes are

---

[5] John C. B. Webster, *The Pastor to Dalits* (Delhi: ISPCK, 1995), 2. The reference was to their writings about teacher-catechists, whom they regarded as the key to mass movement work among Dalits, but applies more generally to all congregations, whether Dalit or not.

important indicators of upward mobility as well as of current problems of overcrowding.

Local lore seems to be the least used source in these essays. That could well be because there is so little of it in the particular localities under study here. That in itself could be evidence of how important Christianity has become to the present generation of Dalit Christians. Nonetheless, P. Dayanandan does refer to it at the outset of his essay, particularly as it affected him personally; he also tapped the memories of his informants for more of it.

The interview is, perhaps the most important primary source of all. This is most apparent in the essays by Godwin Shiri as well as by Raj Kumar Hans and Siddhi Macwan. In their cases the interview seemed to play the leading role and was backed up by other forms of evidence, whereas the other authors tended to use interviews to supplement or fill in the gaps in the information provided by other sources. There is certainly no hard and fast rule that written evidence is always better than oral evidence; both obviously need to be evaluated critically, individually and in relation to each other. It is also a very frustrating type of source, not because people are uncooperative but because they simply cannot remember. For example, the assumption that a community's conversion is such an important event in their shared lives that stories of it would be passed on from one generation to the next simply does hold up in many cases. Memories may go back only a single generation and in a very selective manner. There is also the fact that deliberate attempts were made *not* to pass on information about the past; it is a time best forgotten because it is too painful to recall and may hinder the family's future progress. It is in working with this kind of evidence, whether gathering it or assessing its reliability and significance, that the historian must use the skills of the anthropologist as well as those being developed in the area of oral history.

Several important procedural issues arose in the discussion of the authors' experience with interviews. One such concern was that of identifying those people in the community who know and remember its past. Usually investigators are referred to the elderly it may in fact turn out to be a somewhat younger person who, for family reasons, is even more familiar with the community's history and lore. The pastor may also have picked up quite a bit of it in the process of becoming acquainted with the congregation. It was found that if the investigator was familiar with the contents of the available written records prior to the interview, then that information could be used to help jog the memories of those being interviewed. One author found it best to conduct the initial interview in an informal, casual way that allowed the informants just to share what they remembered in their own way without trying to impose a more structured interview schedule on them. Only at a later stage, when the interviewer had a better sense of the people's history, did a more structured interview become helpful. My own experience as an outside investigator has been that the interview often can become a semi-public event where people gather around to listen and to interject their own observations. These events can lead to intense discussions when disagreements occur. Depending upon the situation and the matter under discussion, the investigator may have to decide whether at least a minimal consensus can be reached or, if not, simply struggle to maintain some sort of focus in a multi-lateral conversation.

One of the most intriguing questions to emerge from this brief discussion of sources is the extent to which the presence or absence of different types of sources not only shape what the historian writes but virtually determines what the central themes of that history will be. In one paper about a Christian village not presented here, the early missionary records focused on the land far more than on the congregation, and indeed relationships to the land became the central theme of that history. Oral history is shaped by what people have managed or chosen to remember from the past, without any independent check on how accurate their memories actually are. For that reason, or because people have forgotten the past, there are probably many Dalit Christian congregations and communities whose histories simply cannot be written; there is just not enough evidence to go on. Thus the historian has to select those which have enough diverse sources to make reconstructing the past a real possibility.

CONTEXT

No local Dalit Christian community or congregation lives as a completely self-contained island totally cut off from the rest of society. Distinctions, boundaries, and forms of separation do exist between them and others, but not isolation. They are connected to the wider society in a variety of ways, e.g., as workers and consumers; as citizens and voters; as creators, sustainers and victims of shared culture; as members of the wider Church. It is therefore impossible to understand them apart from the broader contexts in which they live and to which they are connected. In the preceding chapters, context has been used in at least three important ways in order to deepen understanding of local Dalit Christian history.

The first is that the outsider is often used as a source of information about the local Dalit Christian church or community. Thus the context provides sources of direct information about the group under study and what outsiders have to say about the church or community is part of its history. This is most obvious in the case of the missionary who is an outsider and whose reports, descriptions, and therefore whose views have proved to be integral to as well as indispensable for understanding the early history of Dalit congregations, e.g., in Delhi and in the Chengalpattu area. It was also the missionary outsider who provided and kept all the church registers of various kinds which have been used throughout this book to provide data on social mobility. Hans and Macwan went beyond this most obvious outside source to interview, not just the Christians, but also some of the other residents of Bhalej, and used their observations as a sort of "reality test" to determine whether the self-perceptions of the Bhalej Christians were simply self-serving or were shared by others in the village. More indirectly but no less importantly, Shiri has shown how important the positive views of others have been to the self-image of the Mandya Christians and how this has shaped much of the current direction of their history.

Context has also played an important role in providing explanations of important past events and processes of change. With rare exceptions, the sources of local Dalit Christian history are relatively few and fragmentary. Thus the gaps in the knowledge and understanding they provide are apt to be quite large. "Circumstantial evidence" drawn from the wider contexts in which local Dalit congregations and communities are situated may help to narrow some of those gaps. The preceding chapters provide many examples of this use of context. P. Dayanandan was interested in why the social mobility of the Christians in Andreyapuram and the surrounding villages was so limited. He then went into an extensive examination not only of the previous policies, programmes and conversions of the Scottish mission, but also of the views other missionary contemporaries–especially the highly influential Principal of Madras Christian College, William Miller–towards the higher education of Dalit Christians. Shiri keeps constant track of the employment opportunities open to Dalit Christians in order to understand what has made mobility possible among them. Oommen states quite explicitly that circumstantial evidence and his own knowledge of the locality helped him trace the origins of the Kottankudi congregation. Daniel turned to urban development to explain changes in the homes within the Dalit Christian *basti* at Turkman Gate in Delhi as well as the increased number of people who live there.

More often, however, historians use context to give meaning to or highlight the significance of the information which the sources provide directly. This historians generally do by making comparisons between the group they are studying and other groups within their relevant contexts (e.g., Christian Dalits and other Dalits or other Christians) which reveal either something quite distinctive or something which follows broader current trends. For example, Dayanandan compares the social mobility of upper caste Christians who went to Madras Christian College with that of the Dalit Christians who were not allowed in, thus highlighting the deprivation of the latter. Shri, Oommen, Hans and Macwan use the impact of the government's reservation policy upon the prospects of Christian Dalits to highlight their current economic dilemma as compared with that of other Dalits.

As these examples indicate, the contexts in which any given Dalit Christian community lives are multiple: the village or *basti,* the caste or *jati*, the wider Christian community, the broader Dalit movement, the regional economy, government plans and policies, local or even national party politics. While multiplicity of contexts is recognized and built into all the preceding chapters, there is in each chapter one context which has a certain primacy over the others. In Dayanandan's it is the context of the wider Christian mission; in Shiri's it is the context of the changing economy in the region; in Oommen's it is the broader Pulaya caste context; for Hans and Macwan it is the village context; for Daniel it is the context of political change from Raj to Independence and from the Congress to the BJP.

As these three uses of context indicate, choice and use of context play a significant role in shaping the final interpretation of the past an historian arrives at. Choice and use of context are in turn influenced by the initial standpoints from which historians look at and question both the sources available to them and the multiple contexts in which Dalit Christians have lived, while the sources themselves quite well determine which contexts prove to have been most influential and how they will probably have to be used in order to reconstruct the past. Thus, in local Dalit Christian history, as in other forms of history, sources, historiography and context become closely interconnected as sources of knowledge in the process of investigating and writing about the past.

HISTORIOGRAPHY

As indicated in the introduction to this book, there is a growing body of historical writing on Dalit Christians in several parts of the country. Many of those studies written in English are listed in the bibliography at the end of this chapter. While these neither have the local congregation as their primary focus nor anticipate everything which may turn up in its history, they are nevertheless a useful resource for writing local Dalit Christian history. What they offer initially are some promising questions to ask of the available sources and some fruitful lines of inquiry to pursue when interrogating them.

When the editors sent out their initial letter inviting others to participate in the seminar which produced this book, they offered a list of questions, derived from their knowledge of the kind of Dalit Christian history that has already been written, which not only expressed some common concerns behind the seminar but also could serve as stimuli to the participants' research. The list is a lengthy, but by no means an exhaustive one; it is worth recording here because it sheds some light not only on the preceding chapters but also on our general approach to local Dalit Christian history. These questions, which applied to women as well as to men, were the following. (1) What were the caste and occupational backgrounds of the first generation of converts? (2) How many people were in that first generation of converts? (3) Following conversion, what kind of continuing relationships did they have with those members of their local *jati* who did not convert? What kinds of non-Christian practices did they continue to observe? In short, what kinds of life-style changes accompanied conversion and what kinds did not? (4) What kind of economic resources did the converts have available to them (e.g., land, etc.)? What happened to any land, or other economic resources, the missionaries got for them? (5) Did the mission provide a school or church building for this group of new Christians? (6) What were some of the major aspects of their pre-existing belief systems, particularly as found through their folk traditions, stories and songs? Did their beliefs play a significant role in the conversion process and in their subsequent Christian life? Why? (7) As you examine family histories over the generations, what kinds of experiences of social mobility, if any, did they have? How widespread was this and were there any discernable patterns to it? (8) Are there many examples of individual Christians or Christian families migrating out of or into the particular location you are studying? When and why and to what extent did this happen? (9) Do you notice any changes from one generation to the next with reference to questions 1-8? How do you explain the continuities and changes? (10) What is the history of pastoral care in this location? For example, was there a resident pastor or catechist from the beginning, how often did pastors or missionaries or bishops, etc., come to visit? How often was holy communion served? What kind of things did the catechists or pastors do as part of their pastoral responsibilities? Did any of these change over time from one generation to the next? (11) Did cases of reconversion or change of denomination occur and why?

This list of questions reveals at least two sets of preferences or biases. The first is a preference for regional history. While directed towards local Dalit congregations and communities, these questions are derived from the study of regional histories and reflect a desire to find out whether certain broader regional patterns and trends also exist within the localities under study. Such a preference is almost inevitable among historians whose reading and writing has been focused upon the regional and national rather than the local. This approach has much to commend it. It directs attention towards what either conforms to or deviates from broader patterns and trends, but at the same time it can also divert attention away from what may be quite unique to the experience of a particular local community. The other preference is for what might be called a social history approach to the study of Dalit Christian history. In this approach the congregation is viewed as a social unit; both certain features of the internal life of this social unit (e.g., religious beliefs, celebrations) and its changing relationships to other social units are then examined within the wider, basically social, context of the village, town, city, or denomination.

The preceding chapters show how selectively the authors have used that list of questions. No question was totally ignored, but certainly social mobility was a central theme running through all the chapters. Several authors used occupational data from church registers to see what kind of occupational mobility and consequent rise in social status had been achieved. P. Dayanandan showed how missionaries both promoted and limited social mobility. In three chapters the authors discussed the effects upon the local community's social mobility and status, which the government policy of denying them Scheduled Caste benefits and offering them Backward Class status has had. Daniel shows how the church building itself has enhanced the congregation's status. Beyond the shared theme of social mobility, each chapter has its own emphasis.

Education is Dayanandan's special concern. Shiri as well as Hans and Macwan highlight not only the kind of piety that developed in the Mandya and Bhalej congregations, but also the socio-political consequences of that kind of piety, while Oommen discusses liturgical patterns in relation to prior beliefs and sense of community. An important theme set early in Daniel's chapter is the converts' relationship to their unconverted caste fellows.

At the same time, each of the authors went beyond the list of suggested questions either by refining those questions so as to give them greater specificity or by pursuing fresh questions raised by the sources they were consulting. It is impossible to make quick generalizations about missionary attitudes towards Dalits after reading Dayanandan's chapter, which reveals such opposing views held by members of the same mission. Shiri's chapter raises questions about the cultural medium of Christian worship, especially with regard to music. In a somewhat different way, Oommen raises the issue of what might be called "church culture" (Church of South India vs. Pentecostal) and lifestyle. Hans and Macwan's chapter provokes questions about relationships between different churches within the same village as well as about the impact of emigration upon the church and community which remains in the village. Daniel points to the impact of a changing political climate and changing urban demographics upon a congregation, as well as to the shift from a dependent, receiving congregation to an independent, giving congregation within the diocese. Oommen, in his introduction to the book as a whole, mentioned four themes (memory, identity, mobility, and fragility) emerging from these chapters, not all of which had been anticipated in the original set of suggested questions. In short, studying the history of one local congregation and community can, in its turn, contribute not only data but also new research questions and lines of inquiry to the study of regional and national Dalit Christian history.

This suggests that it is not necessary for local Dalit Christian history to be intellectually derivative from or totally dependent upon regional and national history. Questions and lines of inquiry may emerge from the congregation itself without any awareness at all of other studies of Dalit Christian history. A useful resource for those who prefer to adopt a local congregational approach to the study of local Dalit Christian history is the *Handbook for Congregational Studies* first published in 1986[6] and then substantially revised and published in 1998 under a new title, *Studying Congregations: A New Handbook.*[7] While intended for the study less of the history than of the present state of a congregation in order to provide a base point from which to develop plans for the future, these handbooks describe ways of studying congregations that open up some new lines of inquiry to the historian. Each of the handbooks offers four different perspectives, "frames" or "lenses" for examining congregations, which did undergo some shifts between 1986 and 1998 but can be summarized briefly here.[8]

All of the preceding chapters utilize the lens of social context, "the setting, local and global, in which a congregation finds itself and to which it responds,"[9] as this perspective is characteristic of the social history approach referred to above. The handbooks, however, isolate three levels of context: the demographic character of the neighbourhood, social interaction within the community itself, and the "social worlds" or the socially constructed "perceptions of reality that inform people's daily lives"[10] of the community residents. This third level did not receive its due in the preceding chapters. It is very difficult to enter into the subjective social worlds of past generations, especially if they left no written

[6] Jackson W. Carroll, Carl S. Dudley, and William McKinney, eds., *Handbook for Congregational Studies*, Nashville: Abingdon Press, 1986.

[7] Nancy T. Ammerman, Jackson W. Carroll, Carl S. Dudley, and William McKinney, eds., *Studying Congregations: A New Handbook*, Nashville: Abingdon Press, 1998.

[8] Besides elaborating on these perspectives, the handbooks also offer practical suggestions on how to gather and analyze data in local congregations.

[9] *Handbook for Congregational Studies*, 12.

[10] *Ibid.*, 51.

records behind. However, it is important to find ways to do so because an understanding of their perceptions, values and meaning systems does offer valuable insights into, for example, their changing theological outlooks and forms of piety.

In this book the lens of identity, "that persistent set of beliefs, values, patterns, symbols, stories and style that make a congregation distinctly itself,"[11] has been used more with reference to local Dalit Christian communities than to congregations, even when community and congregation completely overlap. By contrast, the lens of process has hardly been used at all here. This lens focuses upon the formal and informal, internal social dynamics of a congregation through which it "translates faith into common life."[12] A congregation's social dynamics are revealed in the processes through which decisions get made and implemented, leaders are selected and exercise leadership, and people respond to moments of stress and conflict within the congregation. Like its "social world," a congregation's past social dynamics, especially its informal processes, are not easy for the historian to discern, but they are nonetheless a central feature of its internal history.

Program was the fourth lens or perspective mentioned in the 1986 Handbook, but the 1998 Handbook subsumed that under the category of "culture and identity" and substituted resources as its fourth lens. This lens focuses on the "capital" a congregation has to accomplish its chosen tasks. This might include such "hard" resources as money, people, buildings, and pastors as well as such equally important but more "soft and relational" resource as "shared experiences of coming through difficult times, connections to other institutions, and the strength of members' commitment to the congregation."[13] Both the program and resource lenses have been utilized in the preceding chapters, most obviously in Monodeep Daniel's history of the Holy Trinity Church, but it can be difficult for the historian to assess the "softer" resources of earlier

---

[11] *Ibid.*, 12.

[12] Carl S. Dudley, "Process: Dynamics of Congregational Life," in *Studying Congregations*, 105.

[13] William McKinney *et al.*, "Resources," in *ibid.*, 132.

generations unless there happens to be some unusually helpful missionary records available.

Whether the historian chooses to start with the local congregation and community itself or to move to the local from the regional and national (as the contributors to this book have done), there are good resources available to help shape perspectives, frame questions, and develop lines of inquiry. The field is not so new that one must venture into totally unknown territory with nothing to guide one's investigations. Of course, in the process of interrogating sources and contexts, perspectives may shift, questions get revised, and lines of inquiry altered in the light of what one finds. To cite an extreme example, the process perspective may open up exciting possibilities for a new and valuable kind of local Dalit Christian history, but if the sources for it are not available, then it cannot be written. This will have to be checked out on a case-by-case basis. The point to be emphasized here is that the more aware historians are of the many lenses, regional and local, through which they can view, and thus interrogate, the sources and contexts available to them, the better able they will be to tap the full potential of what those sources and contexts have to offer.

CONCLUSIONS

The purpose of this chapter, like that of the book of the whole, has been not only to inform its readers about local Dalit Christian history but also to enlist, encourage, and assist them in carrying out some research and writing on local Dalit congregations, parishes, and communities on their own and for themselves. It is an exciting and potentially fruitful endeavour for at least two reasons, the first and most obvious being that it will contribute to a more general understanding of the Dalit Christian past. As has been stated earlier, most of what has been written on the subject so far is regional rather than local history. Regional and even national developments will be better understood, as local realities are studied in greater abundance and depth.

The second reason for studying local Dalit Christian history is more practical than academic. As indicated earlier in this chapter, it is essential to understand a congregation's past when planning for its future. How and why it got to where it is today (whether seen from the perspectives of context, identity, process or resources) will help shape what it might become tomorrow. But beneath that analytical and visionary task lies something deeper: the inner spiritual capacity to seek and work for significant change together as a congregation or community. As was noted earlier, a congregation or community's identity is shaped in good part by its history. If that history is neglected or ignored, it can neither help the congregation to get its bearings on the present nor assist it in becoming what it knows itself as of called to be. If that history is remembered, however, it will help the congregation or community towards a clearer and more realistic self-image, towards freedom from damaging false self-images (often based on half-truths or downright lies rooted in past controversy), perhaps towards understanding and resolving some of its inner conflicts, and thus towards moving forward from past realities to creating new realities for new generations to come. This book, and the other studies of Dalit Christian history listed below, indicate that Dalit Christian history is not a history to be ashamed of but a history in which Dalit Christians can take legitimate pride. Moreover, their history can be interpreted theologically so as to become a source of confidence in the Biblical God who has brought them, locally as well as regionally and nationally, from where they once were a century or more ago to where they are now. Such confidence in God can be the basis for hope and hope-inspired action for the future, for the God who has brought local Dalit congregations and communities thus far is the God of the future also who will not abandon them in the midst of whatever present adversity they now face.

RECENT WORKS ON DALIT CHRISTIAN HISTORY

Balasundaram, Franklyn J. *Dalits and Christian Mission in the Tamil Country: The Dalit Movement and Protestant Christians in the Tamil Speaking Districts of Madras Presidency 1919-1939 with Special Reference to London Mission Society Area in Salem, Attur, Coimbatore and Erode*, Bangalore: Asian Trading Corporation, 1997.

Bugge, Henriette. *Mission and Tamil Society: Social and Religious Change in South India (1840-1900)*, Richmond: Curzon Press, 1994.

Bugge, Henriette. "The French Mission and Mass Movements," in Geoffrey A. Oddie, ed., *Religious Conversion Movements in South Asia: Continuities and Change, 1800-1900*, Richmond: Curzon Press, 1997, 97-108.

David, Immanuel. *Reformed Church in America Missionaries in South India, 1839-1938: An Analytical Study*, Bangalore, 1986.

Fernandes, Walter. *Caste and Conversion Movements in India: Religion and Human Rights*, New Delhi, 1981.

Forrester, Duncan B. *Caste and Christianity: Attitudes and Policies on Caste of Anglo-Saxon Protestant Missions in India*, London: Curzon Press, 1980.

Gladstone, J. W. *Protestant Christianity and People's Movements in Kerala*, Trivandrum, The Seminary Press, 1984.

Grafe, Hugald. *History of Christianity in India. Volume IV, Part 2: Tamilnadu in the Nineteenth and Twentieth Centuries*, Bangalore: Church History Association of India, 1990.

Harper, Susan Billington. *In the Shadow of the Mahatma: Bishop V. S. Azariah and the Travails of Christianity in British India*, Grand Rapids: William B. Eerdmans, 2000.

Harper, Susan Billington. "The Politics of Conversion: The Azariah-Gandhi Controversy over Christian Mission to the Depressed Classes in the 1930s," *Indo-British Review*, XV, 147-175.

Hrangkhuma, F. *Christianity in India: Search for Liberation and Identity*, Delhi: CMS/ISPCK, 1998.

Jayakumar, Samuel. *Dalit Consciousness and Christian Conversion: Historical Resources for a Contemporary Debate*, Delhi: ISPCK, 1999.

Juergensmeyer, Mark. *Religion as Social Vision: The Movement against Untouchability in Twentieth Century Punjab*, Berkeley: University of California Press, 1982.

Kananaikal, Jose. *Christians of Scheduled Caste Origin*, New Delhi: Indian Social Institute, 1983.

Kooiman, Dick. *Conversion and Social Equality in India: The London Missionary Society in South Travancore in the 19th Century*, Delhi: Manohar Publications, 1989.

Lobo, Lancy. "Conversion, Emigration and Social Mobility of an Ex-Scheduled Caste from Central Gujarat," *Social Action*, 39 (October-December 1989), 423-437.

Manickam, S. *Studies in Missionary History: Reflections on a Culture-Contact*, Madras: Christian Literature Society, 1988.

Manickam, Sundararaj. *The Social Setting of Christian Conversion in South India: The Impact of the Wesleyan Methodist Missionaries on the Trichy-Tanjore Diocese with special reference to the Harijan Communities of the Mass Movement Area*, Wiesbaden: Franz Steiner Verlag, 1977.

Massey, James. "Christian Dalits in India," *Religion and Society*, XXXVII (September 1990), 40-53.

Massey, James. "Christians in North India: Historical Perspective with Special Reference to Panjab," *Religion and Society*, XXXIV (September 1987), 88-106.

Oddie, G. A. "Christian Conversions in the Telugu Country 1860-1900: A Case Study of One Protestant Indian Movement in the Godavary-Krishna Delta," *Indian Economic and Social History Review*, XII (January-March 1975), 61-79.

Oddie, Geoffrey A. *Hindu and Christian in South-East India*, London: Curzon Press, 1991.

Oddie, G. A. "Protestant Missions, Caste and Social Change in India," *Indian Economic and Social History Review*, VI (September 1969), 259-291.

Oddie, G. A. *Social Protest in India: British Protestant Missionaries and Social Reforms 1850-1900*, Delhi: Manohar, 1979.

Oommen, George. "Communist Influence on Dalit Christians - The Kerala Experience," in Kanichikattil Francis, ed., *Church in Context: Essays in honour of Mathias Mundadan CMI*, Bangalore: Dharmaram Publications, 1996, 31-55.

Oommen, George. "Dalit Conversion and Social Protest in Travancore 1854-1890," *Bangalore Theological Forum*, XXVIII (September-December 1996), 69-84.

Oommen, George. "Strength of Tradition and Weakness of Communication: Central Kerala Dalit Conversion," in Geoffrey A. Oddie, ed., *Religious Conversion Movements in South Asia: Continuities and Change, 1800-1900*, Richmond: Curzon Press, 1997, 79-95.

Prabhakar, M. E. "Caste in Andhra Churches–A Case Study of Guntur District, *Religion and Society*, XXXIX (September 1987), 31-51.

Prabhakar, M. E. "In Search of Roots–Dalit Aspirations and the Christian Dalit Question (Perceptions of the Andhra Poet Laureate, Joshua)," *Religion and Society*, XLI (March 1994), 2-20.

Shiri, Godwin. *The Plight of Dalit Christians—A South Indian Case Study*, Bangalore: Asian Trading Corporation, 1997.

Stock, Frederick and Margaret. *People Movements in the Punjab with special reference to the United Presbyterian Church*, South Pasadena: William Carey Library, 1975.

Sunder Raj, Ebe. *The Confusion Called Conversion*, third edition; Chennai: Bharat Jyoti, 1998.

Webster, John C. B. "Christian Conversion in the Punjab: What Has Changed?" (Forthcoming)

Webster, John C. B. "Christianity in the Punjab," *Missiology*, VI (October 1978), 467-483.

Webster, John C. B. "Christians and Sikhs in the Punjab: The Village Encounter," *Bulletin of the Christian Institute of Sikh Studies*, VI (December 1977), 2-27.

Webster, John C. B. "Christians and the Depressed Classes in the 1930s," in D. N. Panigrahi, ed., *Economy, Society and Politics in Modern India*, Delhi: Vikas, 1985, 313-344.

Webster, John C. B. "Christians, Sikhs and the Conversion of the Dalits," *Dharma Deepika* (June 1998), 23-30.

Webster, John C. B. "Dalits and Christianity in Colonial Punjab: Cultural Interactions," in Judith M. Brown and Robert Eric Frykenberg, eds., *Christians, Cultural Interaction, and India's Religious Traditions,* Richmond, U.K.: Curzon Press and Grand Rapids, Michigan: Eerdmans, 2002.

Webster, John C. B. "Leadership in a Rural Dalit Conversion Movement," in Joseph T. O'Connell, ed., *Organizational and Institutional Aspects of Indian Religious Movements*, Shimla: Indian Institute of Advanced Study, 1999, 96-112.

Webster, John C. B. "Missionary Strategy and the Development of the Christian Community: Delhi 1859-1884," in Selva Raj and Corinne Dempsey, eds., *Popular Christianity in India: Reading between the Lines*, Albany: State University of New York Press, 2002.

Webster, John C. B. *The Christian Community and Change in Nineteenth Century North India*, Delhi: Macmillan, 1976.

Webster, John C. B. *The Dalit Christians: A History*, second edition; Delhi: ISPCK, 1994.

LIST OF CONTRIBUTORS

The Rev. Dr. George Oommen is Professor of History of Christianity at United Theological College, Bangalore.

Dr. P. Dayanandan is Professor of Botany at Madras Christian College, Tambaram.

Dr. Godwin Shiri is Associate Director of the Christian Institute for the Study of Religion and Society, Bangalore.

Dr. Rajkumar Hans is Reader in History at the M. S. University of Baroda, Gujarat.

Ms. Siddhi Macwan is Lecturer in History at Sheth I. C. Kapadia Arts & Commerce College, Bodeli, Gujarat.

The Rev. Monodeep Daniel is a Presbyter of the Delhi Diocese of the Church of North India and a member of the Brotherhood of the Ascended Christ, a religious community in Delhi.

The Rev. Dr. John C. B. Webster is retired and serves as Editor of the Dalit International Newsletter.